"IN THE DAYS OF SERFDOM"
AND OTHER STORIES

"IN THE DAYS OF SERFDOM"
AND OTHER STORIES

LEO TOLSTOY

Translated by Louise and Aylmer Maude

FOREWORD BY MARILYN ATLAS

Pine St. Books

Originally published 1911 by Constable & Co. Ltd.
First Pine Street Books paperback edition published 2002
Foreword copyright © 2002 University of Pennsylvania Press

Printed in the United States of America on acid-free paper

10 9 8 7 6 5 4 3 2 1

Pine Street Books is an imprint of
University of Pennsylvania Press
Philadelphia, Pennsylvania 19104-4011

Library of Congress Cataloging-in-Publication Data

Tolstoy, Leo, graf, 1828–1910
    "In the days of serfdom" and other stories / Leo Tolstoy ; translated
by Louise and Aylmer Maude ; foreword by Marilyn Atlas
        p.   cm.
    ISBN 0-8122-1818-3 (pbk : alk. paper)
    1. Tolstoy, Leo, graf, 1828–1910 —Translations into English. I. Title
II. Maude, Louise, 1855–1839. III. Maude, Aylmer, 1858–1938. IV. Atlas,
Marilyn
PG3366.A13 M3   2002
891.73'3—dc21   2002028506

CONTENTS

FOREWORD
Marilyn Atlas

Today, it is not always clear why we should study Leo Tolstoy, a privileged nineteenth-century count who in later life rejected the value of fiction even though he kept on writing it, who lived one way and preached another, a writer most of us can only read in translation. The answer is simple: Tolstoy has much to teach us about nineteenth-century Russia, about how societies transform themselves, about the impact of war, about intimacy and the human heart, and, of course, about the craft of writing powerful, beautiful, and memorable fiction.

"In the Days of Serfdom" and Other Stories is an excellent introduction to Tolstoy's major themes and styles. The collection, originally published in 1911, consists of a novella, "Polikoúshka; or, In the Days of Serfdom," written in 1863, and five short stories composed in 1905–6. The stories are part of the literary experimentation that was happening in Europe and America at the turn of the twentieth century. Tolstoy experiments with narration, internal monologue, dramatic irony, and sketches; he is

conscious of each story's shape, exploring the relationship between idea and image.

All six of the works in this collection are wonderful
examples of the art of the short story. Their themes are
as various as their styles. "Polikoúshka," the longest,
examines slavery, family, free will, and the corruption of
money. "A Prayer," the shortest, looks at motherhood,
grief, and justice. "Kornéy Vasílyef" concerns jealousy
and cruelty in marriage; "Strawberries" demonstrates
how the upper classes are sickened by their own biases
and greed; "Why?" examines the relationship between
upper class Polish freedom fighters and their Russian
captors; and "God's Way and Man's," an anti-capital
punishment story, offers readers a shifting perspective of
imprisonment, resistance, and spirituality.

Because of their general unavailability, these stories
have been ignored by contemporary scholars and teach-
ers, who, when they write about Tolstoy's short fiction,
choose readily accessible stories such as "Family Happiness," "The Death of Ivan Ilych," "The Kreutzer Sonata,"
and "Master and Man." Now, with the republication of
this volume, they will help change the discussions on
Tolstoy's relationship to modernism, to the use of spaces
and silences, as well as to didactic art. Students, scholars,
and lovers of Tolstoy can examine what and how Tolstoy
wrote before *War and Peace* (1863–69), and *Anna Karen-
ina* (1873–76), and after his 1897 treatise "What Is Art?"

which argues that social effectiveness should be the sole criterion of artistic success. These stories demonstrate that Tolstoy did not really follow his own theories of art as he defined them. His stories remain aesthetic, pleasurable, demonstrating problems, without simple, didactic solutions. Social effectiveness never appears to be Tolstoy's bottom line, so, while his theory may reject the importance of craft, his craft remains fine, and the stories written after 1897 continue, brilliantly, to raise as many questions as they answer. *"In the Days of Serfdom" and Other Stories* shows that up until the last decade of his life he wrote fiction not to tell readers what is right and true, but to allow readers to think through the contradictions and complexities of existence.

These stories concern the market economy, shifting values, double consciousness, women's roles and rights, and the hard life of children and idealists. D. H. Lawrence says that Tolstoy has "blood wisdom," and perhaps he is right. In this collection, Tolstoy is not the prophet but the artist, making history palpable and once again alive. Stephen Crane believed that Tolstoy's aim in writing was to make himself good, and in considering these stories we too are made better. These are artistically and historically important stories, helping us become a little closer to a Russia that no longer exists yet directly informs our own lives.

PREFACE

IT is quite common for Russian peasants to bear the names of Greek philosophers or writers, and Polycarp, in its Russianized form of Polikéy, was no unusual name for a serf.

When, as in the title of the first story in this book, the name assumes the form of Polikoúsh-ka, the contemptuously diminutive termination prepares Russians to expect a hero not held in much esteem by his fellows. To English readers the name carries no such premonitory suggestion, and a sub-title, such as " In the Days of Serfdom," seems therefore desirable to forewarn them of the sort of story they are embarking upon.

Whether that same heading is a quite satisfactory general title for the half-dozen stories which make up this volume (in only two of which do the events narrated clearly date back to pre-Emancipation days) may be open to doubt ; but those who have experienced the difficulty of finding a suitable title for a miscellaneous batch of short stories will not judge the matter harshly.

* * * * *

" Polikoúshka," first published in 1863, two years after the Decree of Emancipation, is the only work of Tolstoy's that can be fairly called an anti-slavery story. It was not his way to be enthusiastic about reforms that were popular and widely supported. By the time the mass of educated men began to praise any movement, Tolstoy began to suspect it. Perhaps that was partly why, as a young man, he was half-hearted about the Emancipation, and why, in later life, he was bitterly contemptuous of the Hague Conference, and treated the establishment of Constitutional Government ironically. Moreover, serfdom, as he knew it in his youth, did not seem to him to work much worse than the industrialism and landlordism that existed in his later years. The majority of Russian serf-proprietors were not intentionally cruel, however grossly incompetent they may have been ; and serfdom—under kindly, well-meaning people, such as his ancestors the Gortchakófs and Volkónskys, or under the members of his own family—had much to mitigate its evils. In his family memoirs many cases are recorded of devotion shown by serfs towards their masters, and of kindness shown by masters to their serfs. The clear and definite relationship in which serf and proprietor stood to one another eliminated many causes of misunderstanding that crop up where master and workman both possess rights the exact extent of which is not well-defined. The owner could always make life unbearable for the serf; and, for that very reason, when human relations did exist between them, such relations rested on goodwill, and not on a bargain, and the attachment that grew up was often lifelong.

But when one has said all that can be said for it, serfdom remains an evil system; and Tolstoy was so observant and truthful an artist that, despite any hesitation he may have felt about the matter, the truth comes out in his story, as the word of the Lord came out of the mouth of the prophet Balaam.

The proprietress, Polikoúshka's mistress, is a well-meaning and kindly disposed woman. The steward is as good as a man in his position could be expected to be. The peasants are much like other human beings. Even poor

Polikoúshka himself is weak, rather than intentionally wicked, and his misfortunes make us forget his misdeeds. But the inefficiency of the whole system, and the frightful waste of time and effort it involved, is writ large over the narrative, and forms an unanswerable indictment.

*   *   *   *   *

Two matters referred to in the tale call for a word of explanation—namely, the system of recruiting, and the grouping of the families.

A man taken as a soldier in those days went for twenty years, during which time he was almost entirely cut off from his people at home ; and army life was frightfully hard, even compared with a serf's ordinary lot. Under Nicholas I it was, indeed, quite common for soldiers to be flogged to death for very minor offences.

A certain number of recruits were periodically called for from each estate, and the proprietor might either himself decide which men should go, or he might leave the matter for the peasants to decide among themselves. It often happened that a proprietor would send one or more men from among his domestic serfs, and would let the serfs employed on the land choose the remaining number of recruits from among themselves.

It was customary, from motives of economy, to keep families together as much as possible. Frequently a father and mother with two or three married sons and their wives and children would all live together in one house. The human tendency to quarrel generally caused these large serf families to break up as soon as the proprietor allowed this to occur. After they had broken up, to send away to army service the only man in a household, was equivalent to leaving the wife and children destitute, and causing them to become an economic burden on the proprietor instead of being an advantage to him.

On the other hand, large families which had held together (and which, therefore, contained more than one adult worker) naturally resented being called upon to supply recruits while other people, who enjoyed the advantage of separate homes, escaped that terrible service.

*　　　*　　　*　　　*　　　*

A marked difference in style will be noticed between the first story and the other five in this book.

During the first dozen years of his authorship,

Tolstoy produced a number of tales, of which "Polikoúshka" is a good specimen, written with much detail, and not aiming at great conciseness or exceptional simplicity.

In later years brevity, simplicity, and sincerity were the criteria of art Tolstoy acknowledged ; and he then wrote in quite another way. The last five stories in this book (dating from the years 1905 and 1906) are specimens of that later style. He wrote them for the great mass of readers who have not much time or money to spend on literature, and he tried to strip away from his narrative all superfluous details, and to preserve only what was vital and significant.

These later stories tell their tale as simply as possible, and therefore need no explaining. The events are never forced. The feeling of the narrator is not made so prominent as to evoke opposition ; and everywhere the hand of the master is seen in that carefully balanced proportion which is one of the surest signs of technical proficiency.

Only the last of the tales, " God's Way and Man's," calls for any special comment. There, in the form of a story, Tolstoy says what he so often said in didactic articles—namely, that

society can best be reformed by each man
treasuring the spirit of good-will, and that the
cult of anger, violence, or ill-will always does
harm.

He blames the Revolutionaries for being
actuated by anger, and for their violence, and
for the assassination of Alexander II, but he
stops short of explicitly condemning them for
wishing to organize Constitutional Government, and that restraint enables him to hold
the reader's sympathy. His artistic tact causes
him to stop short of saying in the story—what
he frequently said in his essays—that the
organization of Government is necessarily and
always an evil in itself.

The Materialists—with whom he identified
the Revolutionists and the Socialists—over-
simplify by neglecting the profoundest thing
in life—its spiritual side. But Tolstoy over-
simplified equally by supposing that religious
emotion and conviction can do away with the
need for systematic social organization, in-
volving an immense amount of humdrum,
steady, and persistent work.

Tolstoy belonged to the primitive type of
reformers and prophets who are concerned with
the springs of emotion, but neglect or despise

the careful and detailed adaptation of means to ends in the organization of society.

Fortunately, though he was great in both capacities, the story-teller in him was independent of the essayist. As teacher he mapped out the whole of human life, and showed the organic connection of all its activities. Had he succeeded in doing that without any serious admixture of error, he would have been by far the greatest of all didactic writers ; but valuable and stimulating as his essays are, they yet contain certain errors from which his stories—and even his stories with a purpose—are comparatively free.

AYLMER MAUDE.

IN THE DAYS OF SERFDOM

I

POLIKOÚSHKA; OR, IN THE DAYS OF SERFDOM

I

" Just as you please to order, madam ! Only it would be a pity if it's the Doútlofs. They're all good fellows, and one of them must go if we don't send at least one of the domestic serfs," said the steward. " As it is, everyone is hinting at them. . . . But it's just as you please, madam !"

And he placed his right hand over his left in front of him, inclined his head towards the other shoulder, drew in—almost with a smack—his thin lips, rolled up his eyes, and said no more, evidently intending to keep silent for a long time, and to listen without reply to all the absurdities his mistress was sure to utter.

The steward—clean-shaven, and dressed in a long coat of a peculiar steward-like cut—who had come to report to his proprietress that autumn evening, was by origin a domestic serf.

The report, from the lady's point of view, meant listening to a statement of the business done on her estate, and giving instructions for further business. From Egór Miháylovitch's (the steward's) point of view, " reporting " was a ceremony of standing straight on both feet, with turned-out toes, in a corner facing the sofa, and listening to all sorts of chatter unconnected with business, and by different ways and means getting the mistress into a state of mind in which she would quickly and impatiently say, " All right, all right !" to all that Egór Miháylovitch proposed.

Recruiting was the business under considera- tion. The Pokróvsk estate had to supply three recruits. Two of them seemed to have been marked out by Fate itself, by a coincidence of family, moral, and economic circumstances. As far as they were concerned, there could be no hesitation or dispute either on the part of the proprietress, the Commune, or of public opinion. But who the third was to be, was a debatable point. The steward was anxious to defend the Doútlofs (in which family there were three men of an age to be recruited), and to send Poli-

koúshka, a married domestic serf with a very bad
reputation, who had been caught more than once
stealing sacks, reins, and hay; but the proprietress, who often petted Polikoúshka's ragged
children, and improved his morals by exhortations
from the Bible, did not wish to send him. Neither
did she wish to injure the Doútlofs, whom she
did not know and had never even seen. But
somehow she did not seem able to grasp the
fact, and the steward could not make up his
mind to tell her straight out, that if Polikoúshka
did not go, one of the Doútlofs would have to.

" But I don't wish the Doútlofs any ill !" she
said feelingly.

" If you don't, then pay three hundred
roubles for a substitute," should have been the
steward's reply; but that would have been bad
policy.

So Egór Miháylovitch took up a comfortable
position, and even leaned imperceptibly against
the lintel of the door, while keeping a servile
expression on his face and watching the move-
ments of the lady's lips and the flutter of the
frills on her cap, and their shadow on the wall
beneath a picture. But he did not consider it
at all necessary to attend to the meaning of her
words. The lady spoke long, and said much.

A desire to yawn gave him cramp behind his ears, but he adroitly turned the spasm into a cough, and, holding his hand to his mouth, gave a croak. A little while ago I saw Lord Palmerston sitting with his hat over his face while a member of the Opposition was storming at the Ministry, and then suddenly rise, and in a three hours' speech answer his opponent point by point. I saw it and was not surprised, because I had seen the same kind of thing hundreds of times going on between Egór Miháylovitch and his mistress. At last—perhaps he was afraid of falling asleep, or thought she was letting herself go too far—changing the weight of his body from his left to his right foot, he began, as he always did, with an unctuous preface :

" Just as you please to order, madam. . . . Only, the meeting of the Commune is at present being held in front of my office window, and we must come to some conclusion. The order says that the recruits are to be in town before the Feast of Pokróf.* From among the peasants the Doútlofs are being suggested, and there is no one else to suggest. And the Mír does not trouble about your interests. What does it care if it ruins the Doútlofs ? Don't I know what a fight

* Intercession of the Virgin.

they've been having ? Ever since I first had the stewardship they have been living in want. The old man's youngest nephew has scarcely had time to grow up to be a help, and now they're to be ruined again ! And I, as you well know, am as careful of your property as of my own. . . . It's a pity, madam, whatever you're pleased to think ! . . . After all, they're neither kith nor kin to me, and I've received nothing from them. . . ."

" Why, Egór, as if I ever thought of such a thing !" interrupted the lady, and at once suspected him of having been bribed by the Doútlofs.

" . . . Only theirs is the best homestead in the whole of Pokróvsk. They're God-fearing, hard-working peasants. The old man has been thirty years churchwarden ; he doesn't drink nor use bad language ; he goes to church " (the steward well knew with what to bait the hook). " . . . But the principal thing that I would like to report to you is that he has only two sons ; the others are nephews adopted out of charity, and so they ought to cast lots only with the two-men families. Many families have split up because of their improvidence, and their own sons have separated from them, and so they are safe now— while these will have to suffer just because of their charitableness."

Here the lady could not follow at all. She did not understand what he meant by a " two-men family " nor " charitableness." She only heard sounds and observed the nankeen buttons on the steward's coat. The top one, which he probably did not button up so often, was fixed on tightly ; the middle one was hanging by a thread, and ought long ago to have been sewn on. But it is a well-known fact that in a conversation, especially a business conversation, it is not at all necessary to understand what is being said to you, but only to remember what you yourself want to say. The lady acted accordingly.

" How is it you won't understand, Egór Miháylovitch ?" she said. " I have not the least desire that a Doútlof should go as a soldier. One would think that, knowing me as you do, you might credit me with the wish to do everything in my power to help my serfs, and that I don't desire their misfortune, and that I would sacrifice all I possess to escape from this sad necessity and to send neither Doútlof nor Poli- koúshka." (I don't know whether it occurred to the steward that to escape the sad necessity there was no need to sacrifice everything—that, in fact, three hundred roubles would be sufficient ; but this thought might easily have occurred to him.)

" I will only say this : that I will not give up
Polikoúshka on any account. When, after that
affair with the clock, he confessed to me of his
own accord, and cried, and gave his word to
amend, I talked to him for a long time, and saw
that he was touched and sincerely penitent."
("There ! She's off now !" thought Egór Miháylovitch, and began examining the marmalade
she had in a glass of water : was it orange or
lemon ? " Slightly bitter, I expect," thought he.)
" That is seven months ago now, and he has not
once been drunk, and has behaved splendidly.
His wife tells me he is a different man. How can
you wish me to punish him now that he has reformed ? Besides, it would be inhuman to make
a soldier of a man who has five children, and he
the only man in the family. . . . No, you'd
better not say any more about it, Egór !"

And the lady took a sip out of the glass. Egór
Miháylovitch watched the motion of her throat
as the liquid passed down it, and then replied
shortly and dryly :

" Then Doútlof's decided on."

The lady clasped her hands together.

" How is it you don't understand ? Do I
wish Doútlof ill ? Have I anything against him ?
God is my witness, I am prepared to do anything

for them. . . ." (She glanced at a picture in the corner, but recollected that it was not an icon.) " Well, never mind . . . that's not to the point,'' she thought. And again, strange to say, the idea of the three hundred roubles did not occur to her. . . . " Well, what can I do ? What do I know about it ? It's impossible for me to know. Well, then, I rely on you—you know my wishes. . . . Act so as to satisfy everybody and according to the law. . . . What's to be done ? They are not the only ones : everybody has times of trouble. Only, Polikoúshka can't be sent. You must understand that it would be dreadful of me to do such a thing. . . ."

She was roused, and would have continued speaking for a long time had not one of her maid-servants entered the room at that moment.

" What is it, Dounyásha ?"

" A peasant has come to ask Egór Miháylovitch if the Meeting is to wait for him," said Dounyásha, and glanced angrily at Egór Miháylovitch. (" Oh, that steward !" she thought ; " he's upset the mistress. Now she'll not let one get a wink of sleep till two in the morning !")

" Well then Egór, go and do the best you can."

" Yes, madam." He did not say anything

more about Doútlof. " And who is to go to the fruit merchant to fetch the money ?"

" Has not Peter returned from town ?"

" No, madam."

" Could not Nicholas go ?"

" Father is down with backache," remarked Dounyásha.

" Should I go myself to-morrow, madam ?" asked the steward.

" No, Egór ; you are wanted here." The lady pondered. " How much is it ?"

" Four hundred and sixty-two silver roubles."

" Send Polikoúshka," said the lady, with a determined glance at Egór Miháylovitch's face.

Egór Miháylovitch stretched his lips into the semblance of a smile, but without unclosing his teeth, and the expression of his face did not change.

" Yes, madam."

" Send him to me."

" Yes, madam ;" and Egór Miháylovitch went to his office.

II

Polikéy (or Polikoúshka, as he was usually contemptuously called), as a man of little importance, of tarnished reputation, and not a native of the village, had no influence either with the house-keeper, the butler, the steward, or the lady's-maid. His cubicle was the very worst, though his family consisted of seven persons. The late proprietor had had these cubicles built in the following manner :

In the middle of a brick building, about twenty-three feet square, was placed a large brick baking-oven, partly surrounded by a passage, and the four corners of the building were separated from the " collidor " (as the domestic serfs called it) by wooden stable-partitions. So there was not much room in these cubicles, especially in Polikéy's, which was nearest to the door. The family bed, with a quilt and pillow-cases made of print, the baby's cradle, and the three-legged table (on which the cooking and washing were done and all sorts of domestic articles placed, and at which Polikéy — who was a farrier—worked), tubs, clothing, some chickens, a calf, and the seven members of the family, filled the whole cubicle, and could not have moved in it had it not been for their quarter of the brick oven (on which both people and things could lie) and for the possi-bility of going outside into the porch. That was, perhaps, not easy, for it is rather cold in October, and the seven of them only possessed

one sheepskin cloak between them; but, on the
other hand, the children could keep warm by
running about, and the grown-ups by working,
and both the one and the other by climbing on
to the top of the oven, where the temperature
rose to 120 degrees. It may seem dreadful to
live in such conditions, but they did not mind—
it was quite possible to live. Akoulína washed
and sewed her husband's and her children's
clothes, spun, wove and bleached her linen, cooked
and baked in the common oven, and quarrelled
and gossiped with her neighbours. The monthly
allowance of meal sufficed not only for the
children, but to add to the cow's food. The
firewood was free, and so was food for the cattle,
and a little hay from the stables sometimes came
their way. They had a strip of kitchen garden.
Their cow had calved, and they had their own
fowls. Polikéy was employed in the stables to
look after two stallions; he bled horses and cattle,
cleaned their hoofs, operated on them for lampers,
dispensed ointments of his own invention, and for
this was paid in money and in kind. Also some
of the proprietress's oats used to remain over,
for two measures of which a peasant in the village
gave twenty pounds of mutton regularly every
month. Life would have been quite tolerable,

had there been no worry. But the family had a great grief. Polikéy in his youth had lived at a stud-farm in another village. The stud-groom into whose hands he happened to fall was the greatest thief in the neighbourhood, and got exiled to Siberia. Under this man Polikéy served his apprenticeship, and in his youth got so used to those tricks that in later life, though he would willingly have left them off, he could not get out of the habit. He was a young man, and weak; he had neither father nor mother nor anyone else to teach him. Polikéy liked drink, and did not like to see anything lying about. Whether it was a strap, a piece of harness, a padlock, a bolt, or a thing of greater value, Polikéy found some use for everything. There were people everywhere who accepted these things, and paid for them in drink or in money. Such earnings, so people say, are the easiest to get : no apprenticeship required, no labour nor anything, and he who has once tried that kind of work does not desire any other. It has only one drawback : although you get things cheap and easily, and live pleasantly, yet all of a sudden—through somebody's malice— things go all wrong, the trade fails, everything has to be accounted for at once, and you rue the day you were born.

And so it happened to Polikéy.

Polikéy married, and God gave him joy. His wife, the daughter of a herdsman, turned out to be a healthy, intelligent, hard-working woman, who bore him one fine baby after another. And though Polikéy did not give up his trade, all went well till one fine day his luck forsook him and he was caught. And it was all about a trifle : he stole some reins from a peasant. He was found out, beaten, the proprietress was told of it ; and he was watched. He was caught a second and a third time. People began to taunt him, the steward threatened to make him go as a soldier, the proprietress gave him a scolding, and his wife wept and was broken-hearted. Everything went wrong. He was a kind-hearted man ; not wicked, but only weak; liking drink, and so in the habit of it that he could not leave it off. Sometimes his wife would row at him and even beat him when he came home drunk, and he would cry, saying : " Unfortunate man that I am, what shall I do ? Blast my eyes, I'll leave it off ! Never again !" A month goes by, and he leaves home, gets drunk, and is not seen again for a couple of days. And his neighbours say : " He must get the money somewhere to go on the spree with !"

His latest trouble had been about the office clock. There was an old clock there that had not been in working order for a long time. He happened to go in at the open door all alone, and the clock tempted him. He took it and got rid of it in the town. As ill-luck would have it, the shopman to whom he sold the clock was related to one of the domestic serfs; and coming to see her one holiday, spoke about the clock. They—especially the steward, who disliked Polikéy—began making inquiries, just as if it was anybody else's concern ! It was all found out and reported to the proprietress, and she sent for him. He at once fell at her feet and pathetically confessed everything, just as his wife had told him to do. He carried out his instructions very well. The proprietress began admonishing him ; she talked and talked, and maundered on about God and virtue and a future life, and about wife and children, and at last drove him to tears. She said :

"I forgive you; only you must promise never to do it again !"

"Never in all my life. May I go to perdition ! May my bowels gush out !" said Polikéy, and wept touchingly.

Polikéy went home, and for the rest of the

day lay on the oven, blubbering like a calf. Since then nothing more had ever been traced to him. Only his life was no longer pleasant; he was looked upon as a thief, and when the time for conscripting drew near, everybody hinted at him.

Polikéy was a farrier, as already mentioned. How he became one nobody knew, he himself least of all. At the stud-farm, when he worked under the head-groom who got exiled, his only duties were to clean the stables, sometimes to groom the horses, and to carry water. So he could not have learned his trade there. Then he became a weaver; after that he worked in a garden, weeding the paths; then he was condemned to break bricks for some offence; then he went into service with a merchant, paying a yearly fine to his proprietress for permission to do so. So evidently he could not have had any experience as a veterinary; yet somehow during his last stay at home, his reputation as a wonderfully and even a rather supernaturally clever farrier began gradually to spread. He bled a horse once or twice; then threw one down and prodded about in its thigh, and then demanded that it should be placed in a stall, where he began cutting its frog till it bled. Though the horse struggled, and even squealed, he said this

meant " letting out the sub-hoof blood " ! Then
he explained to a peasant that it was absolutely
necessary to let the blood from both veins, " for
greater lightness," and began hammering in the
blunt lancet with a mallet ; then he bandaged
the innkeeper's horse under its belly with the
selvedge torn from his wife's shawl, and at last
he began to sprinkle all sorts of sores with vitriol,
to drench them with something out of a bottle,
and sometimes to give internally whatever came
into his head.   And the more horses he tormented
and killed, the more he was believed in, and the
more of them were brought to him.

I feel that for us educated people it would
hardly be proper to laugh at Polikéy.   The
methods he employed are the same that have in-
fluenced our fathers, that influence us, and will
influence our children.   The peasant lying prone
on the head of his one mare (which not only
constitutes the whole of his wealth, but is almost
one of his family) and gazing with faith and
horror at Polikéy's frowning look of importance and thin arms with upturned sleeves, as,
with the healing rag or a bottle of vitriol
between his teeth, the latter presses the sore
place and boldly cuts into the living flesh (with
the secret thought, " The one-eyed brute will

never get over it!") and at the same time pretending to know where there is blood and where matter, which is a tendon and which a vein—that peasant cannot conceive that Polikéy has lifted his hand to cut, without due knowledge. He himself could not have done it. And once the thing is done, he will not reproach himself with having given permission to cut unnecessarily. I don't know about you, but I have experienced just the same with the doctor, who in obedience to my request was tormenting those dear to me. The lancet, the whitish bottle of sublimate, and the words, " the staggers—glanders—to let blood or matter," etc., do they not come to the same thing as " nerves, rheumatism, organism," etc. ? *Wage du zu irren und zu träumen** does not refer to poets so much as to doctors and veterinary surgeons.

III

On the evening when the village Meeting, in the cold darkness of an October night, was choosing the recruits and vociferating in front of the office, Polikéy sat on the edge of his bed, rubbing down some horse medicine upon the

* " Dare to err and dream."

table with a bottle; but what it was, he himself
did not know. He had there sublimate of mer-
cury, sulphur, Glauber's salts, and some kind
of herb which he had gathered, having once
imagined it to be good for broken wind, and
now considered not useless in other disorders.
The children had already gone to bed—two on
the oven, two on the bed, and one in the cradle
beside which Akoulína sat spinning. The remainder of a candle—one of the proprietress's
candles which had not been put away carefully
enough—was burning in a wooden candlestick
on the window-sill, and Akoulína every now and
then got up to snuff it with her fingers, so that
her husband should not have to break off his important occupation. There existed independent
thinkers who regarded Polikéy as a worthless
farrier and a worthless man. Others, the majority, considered him a bad man, but a great
master of his art ; but Akoulína, though she often
scolded and even beat her husband, thought him
the first among farriers and the first among men.
Polikéy sprinkled some kind of specific on to the
palm of his hand (he never used a balance, and
spoke ironically about the Germans who use
balances : " This is not a pharmacy," he used to
say). Polikéy weighed the specific in his hand

and tossed it up, but there did not seem enough of it, and he poured in ten times as much. "I'll put in the lot," he said to himself. "It will pick 'em up better."

Akoulína quickly turned round at the sound of the autocrat's voice, expecting some order; but, seeing that the business did not concern her, shrugged her shoulders.

"What knowledge! . . . Where does he get it?" she thought, and went on spinning. The paper which had held the specific fell to the floor. Akoulína did not let this pass unnoticed.

"Annie," she cried, "look! Father has dropped something. Pick it up!"

Annie put out her thin little bare legs from under the cloak with which she was covered, slid down under the table like a kitten, and got the paper.

"Here, daddy," she said, and with her little chilled feet darted back into bed.

"Don't puth!" squeaked her lisping younger sister sleepily.

"I'll give it you!" muttered Akoulína; and both heads disappeared again under the cloak.

"He'll give me three roubles," said Polikéy, corking up the bottle. "I'll cure the horse. It's even too cheap," he added, "brain-splitting work ! . . . Akoulína, go and ask Nikíta for a little 'baccy. I'll return it to-morrow ;" and Polikéy took out of his trouser-pocket a limewood pipe-stem which had once been painted, with a mouthpiece of sealing-wax, and began fixing it on to the bowl.

Akoulína left her spindle and went out, managing to steer clear of everything—though this was not easy. Polikéy opened the cupboard and put away the medicine, then tilted a vódka bottle into his mouth, but it was empty, and he made a grimace ; but when his wife brought the tobacco he sat down on the edge of the bed after filling and lighting his pipe, and his face shone with the content and pride of a man who has completed his day's task. Whether he was thinking how on the morrow he would catch hold of a horse's tongue and pour his wonderful mixture down its throat, or considering the fact that a useful person never gets a refusal—" There, now ! Hadn't Nikíta sent him some tobacco ?" —anyhow, he felt happy.

Suddenly the door, hanging on one hinge, was thrown open, and a maidservant from *up there*— not the second maid, but the third, the little one that was kept to run errands—entered the cubicle. (*Up there*, as everyone knows, means the proprietor's house, even if it is situated lower down.) Aksyúta—that was the girl's name—always flew like a bullet, and did it without bending her arms, which, keeping time with the speed of her flight, swung like pendulums, not by her sides, but in front of her. Her cheeks were always redder than her pink dress, and her tongue moved as rapidly as her legs. She flew into the room, and for some reason catching hold of the stove, began to sway to and fro ; then, as if reluctant on any account to bring out more than two or three words at a time, she all of a sudden breathlessly addressed Akoulína as follows :

" The mistress . . . has given orders . . . that Polikoúshka should come this minute . . . orders to come up. . . ."

She stopped, breathing heavily.

" Egór Miháylovitch has been with the mistress . . . they talked about *rickruits* . . . they mentioned Polikoúshka. . . Avdótya Nikoláyevna . . . has ordered you to come this minute . . . Avdótya Nikoláyevna has ordered . . ." again a sigh, " to come this minute. . . ."

For half a minute Aksyúta looked round at Polikéy and at Akoulína and the children—who had put out their heads from under their bedclothes—picked up a nutshell that lay on the

stove, and threw it at little Annie. Then she
repeated :

" To come this minute ! . . ." and rushed out
of the room like a whirlwind, the pendulums
swinging as usual at right angles to the line of her
flight.

Akoulína again rose, and got her husband's
boots—abominable soldier's boots, with holes in
them—and got down his coat and passed it to
him without speaking.

" Won't you change your shirt, Polikéy ?"

" No," he answered.

Akoulína never once looked at his face while he
put on his boots and coat, and she did well not to
look. Polikéy's face was pale, his nether jaw
trembled, and in his eyes there was that tearful,
submissive and deeply mournful look one only
sees in the eyes of kindly, weak, and guilty people.

He combed his hair, and was going out ; but
his wife stopped him, hid the string of his shirt
that hung down from under his coat, and put
his cap on for him.

" What's that, Polikoúshka ? Has the mistress
sent for you ?" came the voice of the carpenter's
wife from behind the partition.

Only that morning the carpenter's wife had
had high words with Akoulína about her pot of

potash* that Polikéy's children had upset, and
at first she was pleased to hear Polikéy being sum-
moned to the mistress : most likely for no good.
She was a cute, diplomatic lady, with a biting
tongue. Nobody knew better than she how to
pay anyone out with a word : so she imagined.

" I expect you'll be sent to town to do the
shopping," she continued. " I suppose a safe
person must be chosen to do that job, so you'll
be sent ! Please buy a quarter of a pound of tea
for me there, Polikéy."

Akoulína forced back her tears, and an angry
expression distorted her lips. She felt as if she
could have clutched " that vixen the joiner's
wife, by her mangy hair." But when she looked
at her children, and thought that they would be
left fatherless and she herself a soldier's wife and
as good as widowed, she forgot the sharp-tongued
joiner's wife, hid her face in her hands, sat
down on the bed, and let her head sink in the
pillows.

" Mammy, you cluth me !" lisped her little
girl, pulling the cloak with which she was covered
from under her mother's elbow.

" If you'd only die, all of you ! I've brought

* Made by scalding wood-ash taken from the stove,
and used for washing clothes.

you into the world for nothing but sorrow !" exclaimed Akoulína, and sobbed aloud, to the joy of the joiner's wife, who had not yet forgotten the potash.

IV

Half an hour passed. The baby began to cry. Akoulína rose and gave it the breast. Weeping no longer, but resting her thin, though still handsome, face on her hand, and fixing her eyes on the last flickerings of the candle, she sat thinking why she had married, wondering why so many soldiers were needed, and also how she could pay out the joiner's wife.

She heard her husband's footsteps ; and, wiping her tears, got up to let him pass. Polikéy entered like a conqueror, threw his cap on the bed, puffed, and unfastened his belt.

" Well, what did she want ?"

" H'm ! Of course ! Polikoúshka is the least among men . . . but when there's business to be done, who's wanted ? Why, Polikoúshka. . . ."

" What business ?"

Polikéy did not hasten to reply. He lit his pipe and spat.

" To go and get money from a tradesman."

" To fetch money ? " Akoulína asked.

Polikéy chuckled and wagged his head.

" Ah ! Ain't she clever at words ? . . . ' You have been regarded,' she says, ' as an untrustworthy man ; but I trust you more than another ' " (Polikéy spoke in a loud voice that the neighbours might hear). " ' You promised me you'd reform ; here,' she says, ' is the first proof that I believe you. Go,' she says, ' to the customer, fetch the money he owes, and bring it back to me.' And I say : ' We all are your serfs, ma'am,' I say, ' and I must serve you as we serve the Lord ; therefore I feel myself that I can do anything for Your Honour, and cannot refuse any kind of job ; whatever you order I will fulfil, because I am your slave.' " (He again smiled that peculiar weak, kindly, guilty smile.) " ' Well, then,' she says, ' you will do it faithfully ? . . . You understand,' she says, ' that your fate depends on it ?'—' How could I help understanding that I can do something ? If they have told tales about me—well, anyone can tell tales about anybody . . . but I never in any way, I believe, have even had a thought against Your Honour . . .' In a word, I buttered her up till my lady was quite softened. . . . ' I shall think highly of you,' she says." (He kept silent a minute, then the smile again appeared on his face.) " I know very well how to talk to the likes of them ! Formerly, when I used to pay for the right to work on my own, one of them would come down hard on me ; but only let me say a word or two . . . I'd butter him up till he'd be as smooth as silk !"

" Is it much ?"

" Three half-thousands of roubles," carelessly replied Polikéy.

She shook her head.

" When are you to go ?"

" ' To-morrow,' she says. ' Take any horse you like,' she says, ' call at the office, and then start, in Heaven's name !' "

" Glory to the Lord !" said Akoulína, rising and crossing herself.

" May God help you, Polikéy," she added in a whisper, so that she should not be heard behind the partition, holding him by his shirt-sleeve. " Polikéy, listen to me ! I beseech you in the name of Christ our God : when you start, kiss the cross and promise that not a drop shall pass your lips."

" A likely thing !" he ejaculated ; " drink when carrying all that money ! . . . Ah ! how somebody was playing the piano up there ! Fine ! . . ." he said, after a pause, and smiled.

" I suppose it's the young lady. I was standing like this, in front of the mistress, beside the what-not, and the young lady was careering away behind the door. She rattled, rattled on, fitting it together so pat ! Oh my ! Wouldn't I like to play a tune ! I'd soon master it, I would. I'm awfully good at that sort of thing. . . . Get me a clean shirt, do, to-morrow !"

And they went to bed happy.

V

Meanwhile the Meeting had been vociferating in front of the office. The business before them was not a trifling one. Almost all the peasants were present. While the steward was with the proprietress they put on their caps, more voices joined in, and they talked more loudly. The hum of the deep voices, at rare intervals interrupted by breathless hoarse and shrill tones, filled the air, and entering through the windows of the proprietress's house sounded like the noise of the distant sea, making her feel a nervous agitation resembling that produced by a heavy thunderstorm—a sensation between fear and discomfort. She felt as if the voices might at any moment grow yet louder and faster, and then something would happen.

"As if it could not all be done quietly, peaceably, without disputing and shouting," she thought, " according to the Christian law of brotherly love and meekness !"

Many voices were speaking at once, but Theodore Resoún, a carpenter, shouted loudest. There were two grown-up young men in his family, and he was attacking the Doútlofs. Old Doútlof was defending himself : he had stepped forward out of the crowd behind which he had at first stood. Now spreading out his arms, now clutching at his little beard, he sputtered and snuffled in such a manner that it would have been hard for himself to understand what he was saying. His sons and nephews—splendid fellows, all of them—stood pressing behind him, and the old man resembled the mother-hen in the game of hawk-and-chickens. The hawk was Resoún ; and not only Resoún, but all the men who had two grown lads in their family, were attacking Doútlof. The point was, that Doútlof's brother had been recruited thirty years before, and that Doútlof wished to be excused therefore from taking his turn with the families in which there were three grown-up young men, and wanted his brother's service in the army to be counted to the advantage of his family, so that it should be given the same chance as those in which there were only two young men; and that these should all draw lots equally, and the third recruit be chosen from among all of them. Besides Doútlof's family, there were four others in which there were three young men, but one was the village elder's family, and the proprietress had exempted him. From the second, a recruit had been taken the year before, and from the remaining families two recruits were now being taken. One of them had not even come to this Meeting, only his wife stood sorrowfully behind all the others, vaguely expecting that the wheel of fortune might somehow turn her way. The red-haired Román, the father of the other recruit, in a tattered coat— though he was not poor—hung his head and silently leant against the porch railing, only now and then attentively looking up at anybody who raised his voice, and then hanging his head again. Misery seemed to breathe from his whole figure. Old Simeon Doútlof was a man to whose keeping anyone who knew him would have trusted hundreds and thousands of roubles. He was a steady, God-fearing, well-to-do man, and was churchwarden. Therefore the predicament in which he found himself was all the more startling.

Resoún the carpenter was a tall, dark man, a riotous drunkard, very smart in a dispute and in arguing with workmen, tradespeople, peasants, and gentlefolk at meetings and fairs. He was quiet now and sarcastic, and from his superior height he was crushing down the spluttering churchwarden with the whole strength of his ringing voice and oratorical talent. The church-warden was exasperated out of his usual sober groove. Besides these, the youngish, round-faced, square-headed, curly-bearded, thick-set Garáska Kopýlof, one of the talkers of the younger generation, was taking part in the dispute. He came next to Resoún in importance. He had already gained some weight at the Meetings, having distinguished himself by his trenchant speeches. Then there was Theodore Mélnitchny, a tall, thin, yellow-faced, round-shouldered man, still young, with a thin beard and small eyes, always embittered and gloomy, seeing the dark side of everything, and often puzzling the Meeting by his unexpected and abrupt questions and remarks. Both these speakers sided with Resoún. Besides these, now and then two chatterers joined in : one with a most good-humoured face and flowing brown beard, called Hrapkóf, who kept repeating the words, "Oh, my dearest friend!" the other, Zhidkóf, a little fellow with a bird-like face, who also kept remarking at every opportunity, "That's how it is, brothers mine!" addressing himself to everybody and speaking fluently, but without rhyme or reason. They both sided first with one and then with the other party, but no one listened to them. There were others like them, but these two, who kept moving through the crowd and shouting louder than anybody and frightening the proprietress, were listened to less than anyone else, and, intoxicated by the noise and shouting, gave themselves up entirely to the pleasure of wagging their tongues.

There were many other characters among the members of the Commune, stern, respectable, indifferent, dismal, or down-trodden ; and there were women standing behind the men, but, God willing, I'll speak of them some other time. The greater part of the crowd, however, consisted of peasants who stood as if they were in church, whispering behind each other's backs about home affairs, about how best to mark the trees in the forest, or silently hoping that the jabbering would soon cease. There were also rich peasants, whose well-being the Meeting could not add to nor diminish. Such was Ermíl, with his broad, shiny face, whom the peasants called the " full-bellied," because he was rich. Such too was Stárostin, whose face seemed to say, " You may talk away, but no one will touch me ! I have four sons, but not one of them will have to go." Now and then these two were attacked by some independent thinker such as Kopýlof or Resoún, but they replied quietly and firmly, and with a sense of their own immunity. If Doútlof was like the mother-hen in the game of hawk-and-chickens, his lads did not much resemble the chicks. They did not flutter about and squeak, but stood quietly behind him. His eldest son, Ignát, was already thirty ; the second, too, was already a married man, and, moreover, not fit for service ; the third was his nephew Elijah, who had just got married—a fair, rosy young man in a smart sheepskin coat (he was post-horse driver). He stood looking at the crowd, sometimes scratching his head under his hat, as if the whole matter was no concern of his, though it was just him that the hawks wished to swoop down on.

" Why, my grandfather was a soldier," said one, " and so I might in just the same way refuse to draw lots ! . . . There's no such law, friend. Last recruiting, Mihéyevitch was enlisted, and his uncle had then not even returned from service."

" Neither your father nor any uncle of yours has served the Tsar," Doútlof was saying at the same time. " Why, you have not even served the proprietress or the Commune, but spend all your time in the pub. Your sons have separated from you because it's impossible to live with you, so you go suggesting other people's sons for recruits! And I have done police duty for ten years and been churchwarden. Twice I have suffered from fires, and no one helped me over it ; and now, because things go on peaceably and honourably in my homestead, am I to be ruined ? . . . Give me my brother back, then! I dare say he has died in service. . . . Judge righteously, according to God's will, Christian Commune, and don't listen to a drunkard's drivel."

And at the same time Gerásim was saying to Doútlof :

" You are using your brother as an excuse, but he was not enlisted by the Commune. He was sent by the proprietor because of his evil ways, so he is no excuse for you."

Gerásim had not finished when the long, yellow-faced Theodore Mélnitchny stepped forward and began dismally :

" Yes, that's the way ! The proprietors send whom they list, and then the Commune has got to get the muddle straight. The Commune has chosen your lad, and if you don't like it, go and ask the lady. Perhaps she will order me, the one man of the family, to leave my children and go ! . . . There's law for you !" he said bitterly, and, waving his hand, he returned to his former place.

The red-haired Román, whose son had been chosen as a recruit, raised his head and muttered : " That's it, that's it !" and even sat down on the step in vexation.

But these were not the only ones who were speaking all at once. Besides those behind, who were talking about their own affairs, the chatterers did not neglect their part.

" And so it is, faithful Commune," said the little Zhidkóf, repeating Doútlof's words. " One must judge in a Christian manner. . . . In a Christian way, I mean, brothers, we must judge."

" One must judge according to one's conscience, my dear friend," spoke the good-humoured Hrapkóf, repeating Kopýlof's words, and pulling Doútlof by his sheepskin.

" That was the proprietor's will, and not the decision of the Commune."

" That's right! That's what it is," said others.

" What drunkard is drivelling ?" Resoún retorted to Doútlof. " Did you stand me any drinks ? Or is your son, whom they pick up by the roadside, going to reproach me with drink ? . . . Friends, we must decide ! If you want to spare Doútlof, choose not only out of families with two men, but even the one man of a family, and he will have the laugh of us !"

" Doútlof's will have to go ! What's the good of talking ?"

" It's evident the three-men families must be the first to draw lots," began different voices.

" We must first see what the proprietress will say. Egór Miháylovitch was saying that they wanted to send a domestic serf," put in a voice.

This remark stopped the dispute for a while, but soon it flared up anew, and again came down to personalities.

Ignát, whom Resoún had accused of being picked up drunk by the roadside, began to make out that Resoún had stolen a saw from some passing carpenter, and that, when drunk, he had nearly beaten his wife to death.

Resoún replied that he beat his wife, drunk or sober, and still it was not enough ; and this set

everybody laughing.   But about the saw he became suddenly indignant, stepped closer to Ignát
and asked :

" Who stole ? . . ."

" You did," replied the sturdy Ignát, drawing
still closer.

" Who stole ? . . .   Was it not yourself ?"
shouted Resoún.

" No, it was you," said Ignát.

From the saw they went on to a stolen horse, a
bag of oats, some strip of kitchen-garden, a dead
body ; and the two peasants said such terrible
things to one another, that if a one-hundredth
part of them had been true they would at the
very least have legally deserved exile to Siberia.

In the meantime old Doútlof had chosen
another way of defending himself.   He did not
like his son's shouting, and tried to stop him,
saying : " It's a sin. . . .   Leave off, I tell
you !"

At the same time he argued that not only those
who had three young men at home were three-
men families, but also those whose sons had
separated from them.

Stárostin smiled slightly, cleared his throat,
and, stroking his beard with the air of a rich man,
answered that it all depended on the proprietress,

and that evidently his sons had deserved well, since the order was for them to be exempt.

Gerásim answered Doútlof's arguments with respect to the families that had broken up, by the remark that they ought not to have been allowed to break up, as was the rule during the lifetime of the late proprietor ; that it was no use crying over spilt milk ; and that, after all, one could not enlist the only man left in a household.

" Did they break up their households for fun ? Why should they now be completely ruined ?" came the voices of the men whose families had separated ; and the chatterers joined in, too.

" You'd better buy a substitute, if you're not satisfied. You can afford it !" said Resoún to Doútlof.

Doútlof wrapped his coat round him with a despairing gesture, and stepped back behind the others.

" I suppose you've counted my money ?" he muttered angrily. " We shall see what Egór Miháylovitch will say, when he comes from the proprietress."

VI

At that very moment Egór Miháylovitch came out of the house. One cap after another was lifted, and as the steward approached, all the heads—white, grey, red, brown, fair, or bald in front or on top—were uncovered, and the voices were gradually silenced, till at last all was quiet.

Egór Miháylovitch stepped on to the porch, evidently intending to speak. In his long coat, his hands stuffed awkwardly into the pockets, his cap pulled over his forehead, he stood firmly, his feet apart, on this elevated place, lording it over all these heads—mostly old, bearded and handsome—that were turned towards him. He was now a different man from what he had been when he stood before his mistress. He was majestic.

" This is the mistress's decision, lads ! It is not her wish to give up any of the domestic serfs ; but from among you, those whom you yourselves decide on, they shall go. Three are wanted this time. By rights only two and a half are wanted, but the half will be taken into account next time. It comes to the same thing : if it were not to-day, it would have to be to-morrow."

" Of course, that's quite right !" some voices said.

" In my opinion," continued Egór Miháylovitch, " Harúshkin and Váska Mitúhin must go;
that is evidently God's will."

" Yes, that's quite right !" said the voices.

" . . . The third will have to be one of the
Doútlofs, or one out of a two-men family. . . .
What do you say ?"

" Doútlof !" cried the voices. " There are
three of them of the right age !"

And again, slowly, slowly, the shouting increased, and somehow the question of the strip
of kitchen-garden and some kind of sacks stolen
from the mistress's yard came up again. Egór
Miháylovitch had been managing the estate for
the last twenty years, and he was a clever and
experienced man. He stood and listened for
about a quarter of an hour, then he ordered
everybody to be quiet and the three younger
Doútlofs to draw lots, to see which of the three
was to go.

They prepared the lots, which were shaken up
in a hat, and Hrapkóf took one out. It was
Elijah's. All became silent.

" Is it mine ? Let me see !" said Elijah in a
faltering voice.

All remained silent. Egór Miháylovitch gave
orders that everybody should bring the recruiting

money—a tax of seven copecks from every household—next day, and saying that all was finished, dismissed the Meeting. The crowd moved away, the men covered their heads, and as they turned the corner their voices and the sound of their footsteps mingled into a hum. The steward stood on the porch, watching the departing crowd, and when the young Doútlofs had passed him, he beckoned the old man, who had stopped of his own accord, and they went into the office.

" I am sorry for you, old man," said Egór Miháylovitch, sitting down in an arm-chair in front of the table. " Your turn has come. Won't you buy a recruit to take your nephew's place ?"

The old man, without speaking, gave Egór Miháylovitch a significant look.

" He can't escape," said Egór Miháylovitch, in answer to that look.

" We'd be glad enough to buy a substitute, but have not the means, Egór Miháylovitch. Two horses went to the knacker's this summer, and then there was my nephew's wedding. . . . Evidently it's our fate . . . for living honestly. It's very well for him to talk !" (He was thinking of Resoún.)

Egór Miháylovitch rubbed his face with his

hand and yawned. He was evidently tired of the subject ; besides, he was ready for his tea.

"Eh, old fellow ! Don't you be mean !" said he. "Have a hunt in the cellar ; I dare say you'll turn up some four hundred old rouble notes, and I'll get you a substitute—a regular wonder ! . . . The other day a fellow came offering himself."

"In the *government ?*" asked Doútlof, meaning the town.

"Well, will you buy him ?"

"I'd be glad enough, God's my witness ! . . . but . . ."

Egór Miháylovitch sternly interrupted him.

"Well, then, listen to me, old man ! See that Elijah does himself no injury, and as soon as I send word—whenever that may be—he is to be taken to town at once. You will take him, and you will be answerable for him ; but if— which God forbid !—anything should happen to him, I'll send your eldest son instead ! Do you hear ?"

"But could not one be sent from a two-man family ? . . . Egór Miháylovitch, this is an affront !" he said. Then, after a pause, he went on, almost with tears :

"It seems that my brother died a soldier, and now they are taking my boy ! How have I deserved such a blow ?" and he was ready to fall on his knees.

"Well, well, go away !" said Egór Miháylovitch. "Nothing can be done. It's the law. Keep an eye on Elijah : you'll have to answer for him !"

Doútlof went home, thoughtfully tapping the ruts with his stick as he walked.

VII

Early next morning a big-boned bay gelding—for some reason called Drum—harnessed to a small cart (the steward himself used to drive in that cart), stood at the porch of the serfs' quarters. Annie, Polikéy's eldest daughter, barefooted in spite of the falling sleet and the cold wind, and evidently frightened, stood holding the reins at arm's length, and with her other hand held a faded, yellowy-green jacket that was thrown over her head. This jacket served the family as blanket, cloak, hood, carpet, overcoat for Polikéy, and many other things besides. Polikéy's cubicle was all in a bustle. The dim light of a rainy morning was just peeping in at the window, which was broken here and there, and mended with paper. Akoulína went away from her cooking by the oven, and left her children—the youngest of whom were still in bed—shivering because the jacket that served them as a blanket had been taken away and only replaced by the shawl off their mother's head.

Akoulína was busy getting her husband ready for his journey. His shirt was clean, but his boots, which were gaping open, gave her much trouble. She had taken off her thick worsted stockings (her only pair) and given them to her husband, and had managed to cut out a pair of soles from a saddle-cloth (that had been carelessly left about in the stable and brought home by Polikéy two days before) in such a way that they should stop the holes in his boots and keep his feet dry.

Polikéy sat, feet and all on the bed, untwisting his girdle so that it should not look like a dirty rope. The lisping, cross little girl, wrapped in the sheepskin (which though it covered her head was trailing round her feet) had been despatched to ask Níkita to lend them a cap. The bustle was increased by the other serfs, who came to ask Polikéy to get different things for them in town. One wanted needles ; another, tea ; a third, some tobacco ; and another, some oil to burn before his icon. The joiner's wife—who to conciliate Polikéy had already had time to boil her samovár, and bring him a mug full of liquid which she called tea—wanted some sugar.

Though Nikíta refused to lend a cap, and they had to mend their own—*i.e.*, to push in the bits of wadding that hung out of the rents and to sew them up with the surgical needle ; though at first the boots with the saddle-cloth soles would not go on to his feet ; though Annie, chilled through, nearly let Drum get away, and Mary, in the long sheepskin, had to take her place, and then Mary had to take off the sheepskin, and Akoulína had to hold the horse herself—it all ended by Polikéy successfully getting all the warm family garments on to himself, leaving only the jacket and a pair of slippers behind. When ready, he got into the little cart. He wrapped the sheepskin coat round him, shook up the bag of hay at the bottom of the cart, again wrapped himself round, took the reins, wrapped the coat still closer round him in the way that very respectable men do, and started.

His little boy Mike, running out into the porch, begged to have a ride; the lisping Mary also begged that she might " have a lide," and was " not cold even without the theepthkin ;" so Polikéy

stopped Drum and smiled his weak smile, while
Akoulína put the children into the cart and,
bending towards him, asked him in a whisper to
remember his oath, and not to drink on the way.

Polikéy took the children through the village
as far as the smithy, put them down, wrapped
himself up and put his cap straight again, and
drove off at a slow, sedate trot, his cheeks shaking
at every jolt and his feet knocking against the
sides of the cart. Mary and Mike, with their
bare feet, rushed down the slippery hill to the
house at such a rate, and yelling so, that a stray
dog from the village looked up at them and
scurried home with its tail between its legs, which
made Polikéy's heirs yell ten times louder.

It was abominable weather : the wind was
cutting, and something between rain and snow,
and now and then fine hail, beat on Polikéy's face
and on his bare hands which held the reins—and
over which he kept drawing the sleeves of his coat
—and on the leather of the horse-collar, and on the
old head of Drum, who set back his ears and half
closed his eyes.

Then suddenly the rain stopped, and it
brightened up for a moment. The bluish snow-
clouds stood out clear, and the sun seemed to
come out, but uncertainly and cheerlessly, like

Políkéy's own smile. Nevertheless, Políkéy was deep in pleasant thoughts. He whom they threatened to exile and enlist, whom only those who were too lazy did not scold and beat, who was always shoved into the worst places, *he* was now driving to fetch a sum of money, and a large sum, and his mistress trusted him, and he was driving in the steward's cart behind Drum—with whom the lady herself had driven out—just as if he were some innkeeper, with leather collar-strap and reins instead of ropes. And Políkéy settled himself straighter, pushed in the bits of wadding hanging out of his cap, and again wrapped his coat closer.

However, if Políkéy imagined that he looked like a wealthy peasant proprietor, he deluded himself. It is true that everyone knows that tradesmen worth ten thousand roubles drive in carts with leather harness ; only this was not quite the thing. A bearded man in a blue or black coat drives past, sitting alone inside a cart, driving a well-fed horse, and you just glance to see if the horse is sleek and he himself well fed, and at the way he sits, at the horse's harness, and the tyres of the cart-wheels and at his girdle, and you know at once whether the man has a turnover of a hundred or a thousand roubles. Every experienced person looking closer at Polikéy, at his hands, his face, his newly-grown beard, his girdle, at the hay carelessly thrown into the cart, at the bony Drum, at the worn tyres, would know at once that it was only a serf driving past, and not a merchant, or a cattle-dealer, or even a peasant proprietor, and that he was not worth a thousand, or a hundred, or even ten, roubles.

But Polikéy did not think so : he deceived himself, and deceived himself agreeably. Three half-thousand roubles he is going to carry home in the bosom of his coat. If he likes, he may turn Drum's head towards Odessa, instead of towards home, and drive off where Fate will take him. But he will not do such a thing ; he will bring the lady her money all in order, and will talk about having had larger sums than that on him.

When they came to a public-house Drum began to pull against the left rein, turning towards it and stopping ; but Polikéy, though he had the money given him to do the shopping with, cracked the whip above Drum's head and drove on. The same thing happened at the next public-house, and about noon he got out of the cart, and, opening the gate of the tradesman's house where all his proprietress's people put up, led the horse and cart into the yard. There he gave the horse some hay, dined with the tradesman's men, not forgetting to say what important business he had come on, and then went out, with the fruit-seller's bill in the crown of his cap.

The fruitseller (who knew and evidently mis-trusted Polikéy), having read the letter, ques-tioned him as to whether he had really been sent for the money. Polikéy tried to seem offended, but could not manage it, and only smiled his peculiar smile. The fruitseller read the letter over once more, and handed him the money.

Having received the money, Polikéy put it into his bosom and went back to the lodgings. Neither the beershop nor the public-house nor anything tempted him. He felt a pleasant agitation through the whole of his being, and stopped more than once in front of shops exhibiting tempting wares : boots, coats, caps, prints, and food-stuffs, and went on with the pleasant thought : " I could buy it all, but there, now, I won't do it !"

He went to the market for the things he was asked to buy, collected them all, and started bargaining for a tanned sheepskin coat, for which they were asking twenty-five roubles. For some reason the dealer, after looking at Polikéy, seemed to doubt that he could buy it. But Polikéy pointed to his breast, saying that if he liked he could buy the whole shop, and asked to have the coat tried on; felt it, patted it, blew into the wool till he became permeated with the smell of it, and then took it off with a sigh.

" The price does not suit me. If you'll let it go for fifteen roubles, now !" he said.

The dealer angrily threw the coat across the table, and Polikéy went out and cheerfully returned to his lodgings.

After supper, having watered Drum and given him some oats, he climbed up on the oven, took out the envelope with the money and examined it for a long time, and then asked a porter, who knew how to read, to read him the address and the words : " With an enclosure of one thousand six hundred and seventeen Assignation Roubles." The envelope was made of common paper, and sealed with brown sealing-wax, with an anchor stamped on it. There was one large seal in the middle, four at the corners, and there was a drop of sealing-wax near the edge. Polikéy examined all this, and learnt it by heart. He even felt the sharp corners of the paper money. It gave him a kind of childish pleasure to know that he had so much money in his hands. He inserted the money into a hole in the lining of his cap, and

4

lay down with his head on it ; but even in the
night he kept waking and feeling the envelope.
And each time he found it in its place he experienced the pleasant feeling that here was he, the
disgraced, the down-trodden Polikéy, carrying
such a sum and delivering it up so accurately, as
even the steward would not have done.

VIII

About midnight the tradesman's men and
Polikéy were wakened by a knocking at the gate
and the shouting of peasants. It was the party
of recruits from Pokróvsk. There were about
ten of them : Harúshkin, Mitúshkin, and Elijah
(Doútlof's nephew), two reserve recruits, the
village Elder, old Doútlof, and the men who had
driven them. A night-light was burning in the
room, and the cook was sleeping on a bench under
the icons. She jumped up and began lighting
a candle. Polikéy awoke also, and, leaning over
from the top of the oven, looked at the peasants
as they came in. They came in crossing themselves, and sat down on the benches round the
room. They all seemed perfectly calm, so that
one could not tell which of them were being

enlisted and who had them in charge. They
were saying "How d'you do?" talking loudly,
and asking for food. It is true that some were
silent and sad; but, on the other hand, others
were unusually merry, evidently drunk. Among
these was Elijah, who had never had too much
to drink before.

"Well, lads, shall we go to sleep, or have some
supper?" asked the Elder.

"Supper!" said Elijah, throwing open his coat,
and settling himself on a bench. "Send for
vódka."

"Enough of your vódka!" answered the Elder
shortly, and turning to the others he said:

"You just cut yourselves a bit of bread, lads!
Why wake people up?"

"Give me vódka!" Elijah repeated, without
looking at anybody. "I tell you, give me
some!" Then, noticing Polikéy: "Polikéy! Hi,
Polikéy! You here, dear friend? Why, I am
going for a soldier. . . . Have taken final leave
of mother, of my missus. . . . How she howled!
They've bundled me off for a soldier. . . . Stand
me some vódka!"

"I've no money," answered Polikéy, and to
comfort him, added: "Who knows? By God's
help you may be rejected! . . ."

" No, friend. I'm as sound as a young birch. I've never had an illness. There's no rejecting for me! What better soldier can the Tsar want ?"

Polikéy began telling him how a peasant gave the doctor a five-rouble note and got rejected.

Elijah drew nearer the oven, and started talking.

" No, Polikéy, it's all up now! I don't wish to stay myself. Uncle has done for me. As if we could not have bought a substitute ! . . . No, he pities his son, and grudges the money, so they send me. No! I don't want to stay myself." He spoke gently, confidingly, under the influence of quiet sorrow. " One thing only—I am sorry for mother, dear heart ! . . . How she grieved! And the missus, too! . . . They've ruined the woman just for nothing; now she'll perish—in a word, she'll be a soldier's wife ! Better not have married. Why did they marry me ? . . . They'll come here to-morrow."

" But why have they brought you so soon ?" asked Polikéy; " nothing was heard about it, and then, all of a sudden . . ."

" Why, they're afraid I shall do myself some injury," answered Elijah, smiling. " No fear ! I'll do nothing of the kind. I shall not be lost

even as a soldier ; only I'm sorry for mother. . . .
Why did they marry me ?" he said gently and
sadly.

The door opened and banged loudly as old
Doútlof came in, shaking the wet off his cap, and,
as usual, in bark shoes so big that they looked
like boats.

" Athanasius," he said to the porter, when he
had crossed himself, " isn't there a lantern, to get
some oats by ?"

Doútlof, without looking at Elijah, began
slowly lighting a bit of candle. His gloves and
whip were stuck into the girdle tied neatly round
his coat, and his toil-worn face appeared as ordinary, simple, quiet, and full of business cares as
if he had just arrived with a train of loaded carts.

Elijah became silent when he saw his uncle,
and looked dismally down at the bench again.
Then, addressing the Elder, he muttered :

" Vódka, Ermíl ! I want some drink !" His
voice sounded vindictive and dejected.

" Drink, at this time ?" answered the Elder,
who was eating something out of a bowl. " Don't
you see the others have had a bite and gone to lie
down ? Why do you kick up a row ?"

The word " row " evidently suggested to Elijah
the idea of violence.

" Elder, I'll do some mischief if you don't give me vódka !"

" Couldn't you bring him to reason ?" the Elder said, turning to Doútlof, who had lit the lantern and stopped, apparently to see what would happen, and was looking pityingly at his nephew out of the corners of his eyes, as if surprised at his childishness.

Elijah, taken aback, again muttered :

" Vódka !   Give . . . do mischief !"

" Leave off, Elijah !" said the Elder gently. " Really, now, leave off !   You'd better !"

But before the words were out, Elijah had jumped up and hit a window-pane with his fist, and shouting at the top of his voice : " You won't hear me !   So there you are !" rushed to the other window to break that also.

Polikéy, in the twinkling of an eye, rolled twice over and hid in the farthest corner of the top of the oven, so quickly that he scared all the cockroaches there.   The Elder threw down his spoon and rushed toward Elijah.   Doútlof untied his girdle, and shaking his head and making a clicking noise with his tongue, approached Elijah, who was already struggling with the Elder and the porter, who were keeping him away from the window.   They had caught his arms and seemed to be holding him fast ; but as soon as he saw his uncle and the girdle, his strength increased tenfold and he tore himself away, and with rolling eyes and clenched fists stepped up to Doútlof.

" I'll kill you ! Keep away, barbarian ! . . . You have ruined me, you and your brigands of sons, you've ruined me ! . . . Why did they marry me ? . . . Keep away ! I'll kill you ! . . ."

Elijah was terrible. His face was purple, his eyes rolled, the whole of his young, healthy body trembled as in a fever. He seemed to wish and to be able to kill all the three men who were facing him.

" You're drinking your brother's blood, you blood-sucker !"

Something flashed across Doútlof's ever-placid face. He took a step forward.

" You won't take it peaceably !" said he suddenly. The wonder was, where he got the energy ; for with a quick motion he caught hold of his nephew, fell to the ground with him, and, with the aid of the Elder, began binding his hands with the girdle. They struggled for about five minutes. At last, with the help of the peasants, Doútlof rose, pulling his coat out of Elijah's clutch. Then he raised Elijah, whose

hands were bound behind his back, and made
him sit down in a corner on a bench.

"I told you it would be the worse for you,"
he said, still out of breath with the struggle,
and pulling straight the narrow girdle tied over
his shirt.

"What's the use of sinning ? We shall all
have to die ! . . . Fold a coat for a pillow,"
he said, turning to the porter, "or the blood
will get to his head." And he tied the cord
round his waist over his sheepskin, and taking
up the lantern, went to see after the horses.

Elijah, pale, dishevelled, his shirt pulled out
of place, was gazing round the room as if he were
trying to remember where he was. The porter
picked up the broken bits of glass, and stuck a
coat into the hole in the window to keep out the
draught. The Elder again sat down to his bowl.

"Ah, Elijah, Elijah ! I'm sorry for you,
really ! What's to be done ? There's Harúshkin . . . he, too, is married. Seems it can't be
helped !"

"It's all on account of that fiend, my uncle,
that I'm being ruined !" Elijah repeated, dryly
and bitterly. "He is chary of his own ! . . .
Mother says the steward told him to buy a substitute. He won't ; he says he can't afford it.

As if what my brother and I have brought into his house were a trifle ! . . . He is a fiend !"

Doútlof returned, said his prayers in front of the icons, took off his outdoor things, and sat down beside the Elder. The cook brought more kvas and another spoon. Elijah was quiet, and closing his eyes lay down on the folded coat. The Elder, shaking his head silently, pointed to him. Doútlof waved his hand.

" As if one was not sorry ! . . . My own brother's son ! . . . One is not only sorry, but it seems they also make me out a villain towards him. . . . Whether it's his wife . . . she's a cunning little woman though she's so young . . . that has put it into his head that we could afford to buy a substitute ! . . . Anyhow, he's reproaching me. But one does pity the lad ! . . ."

" Ah ! he's a fine lad," said the Elder.

" But I'm at the end of my tether with him ! To-morrow I shall let Ignát come, and his wife wanted to come too."

" All right—let them come," said the Elder, rising and climbing on to the oven. " What is money ? Money is dross !"

" If one had the money, who would grudge it ?" muttered one of the tradesman's men, lifting his head.

" Ah, money, money ! It's the cause of much
sin," replied Doútlof. " Nothing in the world
is the cause of so much sin, and the Scriptures say
so too."

" Everything is said there," the porter agreed.
" There was a man told me how a merchant had
stored up a heap of money and did not wish to
leave any behind ; he loved it so that he took it
with him to the grave. As he was dying he asked
to have a small pillow buried with him. No one
suspected anything, and so it was done. Then
the sons began to search for the money. Nothing
was to be found. At last one of the sons guessed
that probably the notes were all in the pillow.
It went as far as the Tsar, and he allowed the
grave to be opened. And what do you think ?
There was nothing in the pillow, but the coffin
was full of creeping things, and so it was buried
again. . . . You see what money does !"

" It's a fact, it causes much sin," said Doútlof,
and he got up and began to say his prayers.

When he had finished, he looked at his nephew.
The lad was asleep. Doútlof came up to him,
loosened the girdle, and then lay down. One
of the other peasants went out to sleep with
the horses.

IX

As soon as all was quiet, Polikéy climbed down softly, like a guilty man, and began to get ready. Somehow he felt uneasy at the thought of spending the night there among the recruits. The cocks were already crowing more frequently, answering one another. Drum had eaten all his oats, and was straining towards the drinking-trough. Polikéy harnessed him and led him out, past the peasant carts. His cap, with its contents, was safe, and the wheels of his cart were soon rattling along the frozen Pokróvsk road.

Polikéy felt easier only when he had left the town behind. Up to then he kept imagining that at any moment he might hear himself being pursued, that he would be stopped, and that in place of Elijah's arms his own would be bound behind his back, and he would be taken to the recruiting station next morning. It might have been the frost, or it might have been fear; but something made cold shivers run down his back, and again and again he kept touching up Drum with the whip. The first person he met was a priest in a tall fur cap, accompanied by a workman blind in one eye. Taking this for an evil omen, Polikéy grew still more alarmed; but outside the town this fear gradually passed. Drum went on at a walking pace; the road in front became more visible.

Polikéy took off his cap and felt the notes. " Shall I hide it in my bosom ?" he thought. " No ; I should have to undo my girdle. . . . Wait a bit ! When I get to the foot of the incline, I'll get down and arrange myself again. . . . The cap is sewn up tight at the top, and it can't fall through the lining. After all, I'd better not take the cap off till I get home."

When he had reached the foot of the incline, Drum of his own accord trotted up the next hill, and Polikéy, who was as anxious as Drum to get home, did not check him. All was well—at any rate, so Polikéy imagined ; and he gave himself up to dreams of his mistress's gratitude, of the five roubles which she would give him, and of the joy of his family. He took off his cap, felt for the envelope, and, smiling, put the cap tighter on his head. The velveteen crown of the cap was very rotten, and just because Akoulína had carefully sewn up the rents in one place, it burst open in another ; and the very movement by which Polikéy in the dark had thought to push the envelope with the money deeper under the wadding, tore the cap farther, and pushed out a corner of the envelope through the velveteen crown.

The dawn was appearing, and Polikéy, who had not slept all night, began to drowse. Pulling his cap lower down, and thereby pushing the envelope still farther out, Polikéy let his head droop forward towards the front of the cart. He awoke near home, and was about to catch hold of his cap ; but, feeling that it sat firmly on his head, he did not take it off, convinced that the envelope was inside. He gave Drum a touch, arranged the hay in the cart again, put on the appearance of a well-to-do peasant, and, proudly looking about him, rattled homewards.

There was the kitchen ; there the domestic serfs' quarters. There was the joiner's wife carrying some linen cloth ; there was the office, and there the house of the proprietress, where in a few moments Polikéy would be proving himself to be a trustworthy and honest man. " One can say anything about anybody," he would say ; and the lady would reply, " Well, thank you, Polikéy ! Here are three (or perhaps five, perhaps even ten) roubles," and she would order tea for him, or even vódka. " It would not be amiss, after being out in the cold. With ten roubles we would have a treat on the holiday, and buy boots, and return Nikíta his four and a half roubles (it can't be helped ! . . . He has begun bothering). . . ."

When he was some hundred steps from his home, Polikéy wrapped his coat round him, pulled his girdle straight, took off his cap, smoothed his hair, and without haste thrust his hand inside the lining. The hand began to move faster and faster inside the lining, then the other hand went in too, while his face grew paler and paler. One of the hands went right through the cap.

Polikéy fell on his knees, stopped the horse, and began searching in the cart among the hay and the things he had bought, feeling inside his coat and in his trouser pockets. The money was nowhere to be found.

"Dear me !   What does it mean ? . . .   What is going to happen ? . . ." He began howling, clutching at his hair. But recollecting that he might be seen, he turned the horse back, pulled the cap on, and drove the dissatisfied Drum back along the road.

"I can't bear going out with Polikéy," Drum must have thought. "Once in all his life he has fed and watered me at the right time, and then only in order to deceive me so unpleasantly !

How hard I tried to run home ! I am tired, and hardly have we got within smell of our own hay before he starts driving me back !"

" Now then, you devil's jade !" shouted Polikéy through his tears, standing up in the cart, pulling at Drum's mouth and beating him with the whip.

X

All that day no one in Pokróvsk saw Polikéy. The mistress asked for him several times after dinner, and Aksyúta came flying to Akoulína ; but Akoulína said he had not yet returned, and that evidently the customer had detained him, or something had happened to the horse. " If only it has not gone lame !" she said. " Last time, when Maxím went, he was on the road a whole day—had to walk back all the way."

And Aksyúta turned her pendulums in the opposite direction, while Akoulína, trying to calm her own fears, invented reasons to account for her husband's absence ; but in vain. Her heart was heavy, and she could not work with a will at any of the preparations for the morrow's holiday. She was suffering all the more because the joiner's wife assured her that she herself had seen " a man just like Polikoúshka drive up to the avenue, and then turn back again."

The children were also anxiously expecting "Daddy," but for another reason. Annie and Mary, being left without the sheepskin and the coat which made it possible to take turns out of doors, could only run out in their indoor dresses quickly and in a small circle round the house. This was not a little inconvenient for all the dwellers in the serfs' quarters who wanted to go in or out. Once Mary ran against the legs of the joiner's wife, who was carrying water, and though she began to howl in anticipation as soon as she knocked against the woman's knees, she got her hair pulled all the same, and cried still louder. When she did not knock against anyone, she flew in at the door, and, straightway climbing on a tub, got on to the top of the oven. Only the mistress and Akoulína were really anxious about Polikéy ; the children were concerned only about what he had on.

Egór Miháylovitch, in answer to the mistress's questions, " Has Polikoúshka not yet returned ?" and " Where can he be ?" answered : " I can't say," and seemed pleased that his expectations were being fulfilled. " He ought to have been back by dinner-time," said he significantly.

All that day no one heard anything of Polikéy ; only later on it was known that some neighbouring peasants had seen him running about on the road, bareheaded, and asking everybody whether they had seen a letter. Another man had seen him asleep by the roadside, beside a horse and cart tied up. " I thought he was tipsy," the man said ; " and the horse looked as if it had not been fed for two days, its sides were so fallen in."

Akoulína did not sleep all night, and kept listening ; but Polikéy did not return that night. Had she been alone, and had she kept a cook and a maid, she would have felt still more unhappy ; but as soon as the cocks crowed and the joiner's wife got up, Akoulína was obliged to rise and light the fire. It was a holiday. The bread had to come out of the oven before daybreak, kvas had to be made, cakes baked, the cow milked, dresses and shirts ironed, the children washed, and the neighbour not allowed to take up the whole of the oven. So Akoulína, still listening, set to work.

It had grown light, and the church bells were ringing. The children were up, and Polikéy had still not returned. A little snow had fallen the day before, and lay in patches on the fields, on the road, and on the roofs ; and now, as if in honour of the feast, the day was fair, sunny and frosty, so that one could see far and hear far.

But Akoulína, standing by the brick oven, her head thrust into the opening in front, was so busy with her cakes that she did not hear Polikéy drive up, and knew only from the children's shouting that her husband had returned.

Annie, as the eldest, had greased her hair and dressed herself without help.   She wore a new but crumpled print dress—a present from the pro-prietress.   It stuck out as stiff as if it were made of bark, and was a thorn in the neighbours' eyes ; her hair was shining ; she had smeared half an inch of tallow candle on to it.   Her shoes, though not new, were respectable.   Mary was still wrapped in the old jacket, and was covered with mud ; and Annie would not let her come near for fear of getting dirtied.   Mary was out-side.   She saw her father drive up, bringing a sack.

" Daddy has come !" she shrieked, and rushed headlong in at the door, past Annie, dirtying her. Annie, no longer fearing the dirt, went for her at once and hit her.   Akoulína could not leave her work, and only shouted at the children : " Now, then . . . I'll whip you all !" and glowered round at the door.

Políkéy came in with the bag, and at once passed through to his own cubicle.

It seemed to Akoulína that he was pale, and his face looked as if he were either smiling or crying, but she had no time to find out which it was.

" Well, Políkéy, is it all right ?" she called to him from the oven.

Políkéy muttered something that she did not understand.

" Eh ?" she cried. " Have you been to the mistress ?"

Políkéy was sitting on the bed in their cubicle, looking wildly round him, and smiling his guilty, deeply sorrowful smile. He did not answer for a long time.

" Eh, Políkéy ? Why so long ?" came Akoulína's voice.

" Yes, Akoulína, I have handed the lady her money. How she thanked me !" he said suddenly, and began looking round and smiling still more uneasily. Two things attracted his feverishly staring eyes : the baby, and a rope attached to the cradle.

He came up to where the cradle hung, and began hastily undoing the knot of the rope with his thin fingers. Then his eyes fixed themselves on the baby ; but when Akoulína entered, carrying a board full of cakes, Polikéy quickly hid the rope in his bosom and sat down on the bed.

" What is it, Polikéy ? You seem not yourself," said Akoulína.

" Haven't slept," he answered.

Suddenly something flitted past the window, and in a moment Aksyúta, the maid from " up there," darted in like an arrow.

" The mistress orders Polikéy to come this minute," she said—" this minute, Avdótya Nikoláyevna's orders are . . . this minute !"

Polikéy looked at Akoulína, then at the girl.

" I'm coming. What can she want ?" he said, so simply that Akoulína grew quieter. " Perhaps she wants to reward me. Tell her I'm coming."

He rose and went out. Akoulína took the washing-trough, put it on a bench, filled it with water from the pails which stood by the door and from the boiler in the oven, rolled up her sleeves, and felt the water.

" Come, Mary, I'll wash you."

The cross, lisping little girl began howling.

" Come, you slattern ! I'll give you a clean smock. Now then, don't make a fuss ! Come along. . . . I've still your brother to wash."

Meanwhile Polikéy had not followed the maid

from "up there," but had gone to a very
different place. In the passage, by the wall,
was a step-ladder leading to the garret. Polikéy,
when he came out, looked round, and not
seeing anyone climbed that ladder almost at a
run, nimbly and hurriedly.

"What can it mean that Polikéy does not
come?" asked the mistress impatiently of Dounyásha, who was dressing her hair. "Where is
Polikéy? Why has he not come?"

Aksyúta again flew to the serfs' quarters, and
again rushed into the passage, calling Polikéy to
her mistress.

"Why, he went long ago," answered Akoulína,
who, having washed Mary, had just put her
baby-boy into the washing-trough, and was
moistening his thin short hair, regardless of his
cries. The boy screamed, puckered his face, and
tried to catch hold of something with his helpless
little hands. Akoulína supported his plump,
dimpled little back with one large hand, while
washing him with the other.

"See if he has not fallen asleep somewhere,"
said she, looking round anxiously.

Just then the joiner's wife, with her hair un-
done and her dress unfastened, and holding up
her skirts, went up into the garret to get some

things she had hung up to dry there. Suddenly a cry of horror filled the garret, and the joiner's wife, with her eyes closed, came down the steps on all fours, backwards, sliding rather than running, like a madwoman.

" Polikéy ! . . ." she screamed.

Akoulína let go the baby.

" Strangled !" bellowed the joiner's wife.

Akoulína, paying no heed to the baby, who rolled over like a ball and fell backwards, with his little legs in the air and his head under water, rushed out into the passage.

" On a rafter . . . hanging !" the joiner's wife ejaculated, but stopped when she saw Akoulína.

Akoulína darted up the steps, and before anyone could stop her she was at the top ; but from there with a terrible cry she fell back like a corpse ; and would have been killed if the people who had come running from every cubicle had not been in time to catch her.

XI

For several minutes no explanation could be arrived at amidst the general tumult. A crowd of people had collected, everyone was shouting and

talking, children and old women were crying.
Akoulína lay unconscious.

At last the men—the joiner and the steward—
who had run to the place, went up the ladder,
and the joiner's wife began telling for the
twentieth time how she, " nothing doubting,
went to fetch a dress, and just looked—this wise—
and see . . . a man . . . and I look, and a cap is
lying inside-out, close by. I look . . . the legs
are swinging. . . . I went cold all over ! Is it
pleasant ? . . . To think of a man hanging himself, and that I should be the one to see him !
. . . How I came clattering down I myself don't
remember . . . it's a miracle how God saved me !
Really, the Lord has had mercy on me ! . . . Is
it a trifle ? . . . such steepness and from such a
height. . . . Why, I might have been killed !"

The men who had gone up had the same tale
to tell. Polikéy, in his shirt and trousers, was
hanging from a rafter by the rope which he had
unfastened from the cradle. His cap, turned
inside out, lay beside him, his coat and sheepskin
were neatly folded, and lay close by. His feet
touched the ground, but he no longer showed
signs of life.

Akoulína regained consciousness, and again
rushed to the ladder, but was held back.

" Mamma, Syómka's tsoking !" the lisping little girl suddenly cried from their cubicle. Akoulína tore herself away, and ran to her room. The baby did not stir, and his little legs were not moving. Akoulína snatched him out, but he did not breathe or move. She threw him down on the bed, and, with arms akimbo, burst into such loud, ringing, terrible laughter that Mary, who at first had started laughing herself, covered her ears with her hands, and ran out into the passage crying. The crowd thronged into the cubicle, wailing and weeping. They carried out the little body and began rubbing it, but in vain. Akoulína tossed about on the bed, and laughed— laughed so that all who heard her were frightened. Only now, seeing this motley crowd of men and women, old people and children, did one fully realize what a number, and what sort, of people lived in the serfs' quarters. Everybody fussed and spoke ; many wept, but nobody did any-thing. The joiner's wife still found people who had not heard her tale about the way her tender feelings were shocked by the unexpected sight, and how God had saved her from falling down the ladder. An old man who had been a foot-man, with a woman's jacket thrown over his shoulders, was relating how in the days of the old

proprietor a woman drowned herself in the pond.
The steward sent messengers to the priest and to
the policeman, and appointed men to keep guard.
Aksyúta, the maid from " up there," kept gazing
with staring eyes at the opening that led to the
garret, and though she could not see anything,
was unable to tear herself away and go back to
her mistress. Agatha Miháylovna, who had been
lady's-maid to the former proprietress, was weeping and asking for some tea to soothe her nerves.
Anna, the midwife, was laying out the little body
on the table, with her practised, plump, oily
hands. Other women stood in front of Akoulína, silently looking at her. The children, huddled
together in a corner, kept glancing at their mother
and bursting into howls; and then, growing
silent for a moment, glanced again, and huddled
still closer. Boys and men thronged round the
porch, looking in at the door and the windows
with frightened faces; and, unable to see or understand anything, asking one another what it was
all about. One said the joiner had chopped off
his wife's foot with an axe. Another said that
the laundress had borne triplets; a third, that
the cook's cat had gone mad and bitten the
people. But the truth gradually spread, and at
last it reached the proprietress. And apparently

no one understood how to prepare her! That rough Egór blurted the facts straight out to her, and so upset the lady's nerves that it was a long time before she could recover.

The crowd had already begun to quiet down; the joiner's wife set the samovár to boil and made tea; and the outsiders—not being invited—thought it impolite to stay any longer. The boys began fighting outside the porch. Everybody now knew what had happened; and, crossing themselves, they began dispersing, when suddenly a cry was raised:

" The mistress! The mistress!"

And everybody crowded and pressed together to make way for her; but at the same time everybody wanted to see what she would do. The lady, pale and with tear-stained face, entered the passage, crossed the threshold, and went into Akoulína's cubicle. A dozen heads close together gazed in at the door. One pregnant woman was pushed so that she gave a squeak, but made use of that very circumstance to appropriate to herself a front place.

And how could one help wishing to see the lady in Akoulína's cubicle? It was just like the coloured lights at the end of a performance. It must be an important occasion, since they burnt the coloured fires; and so it must be an important occasion when the lady in her silk and lace entered Akoulína's cubicle.

The lady came up and took Akoulína's hand, but Akoulína snatched it away. The old domestic serfs shook their heads reprovingly.

" Akoulína !" said the lady. " You have your children—have pity on yourself !"

Akoulína burst out laughing and got up.

" My children are all silver, all silver ! I don't keep any paper money," she muttered very quickly. " I told Polikéy, ' Take no notes,' and there, now, they've buttered him, buttered him up with tar—tar and soap, madam ! Whatever rash you may have, it will pass at once . . ." and she laughed still louder.

The mistress turned round, and gave orders that the doctor's assistant should come with mustard poultices. " Bring some cold water," she said, and began looking for water herself; but, seeing the dead baby, with Anna the midwife beside it, the lady turned away, and everybody saw how she hid her face in her handkerchief and began to cry; while Anna (it was a pity the lady could not see her—she would have appreciated it, and it was all done for her sake) covered the baby with a piece of linen cloth, put his arms right with her plump, deft hands, shook her head, pouted, drooped her eyelids, and sighed with so much feeling that everybody could see how excellent a heart she had. But the lady did not see it ; she could not see anything. She burst out sobbing, and went into hysterics.

Holding her up under the arms, they led her out into the passage and took her home. " That's all the good she's done !" thought many, and again began to disperse.

Akoulína went on laughing and talking nonsense. She was taken into another room and bled, and plastered over with mustard poultices, and ice was put on her head ; but she did not come to her senses, and did not cry, but laughed, and kept doing and saying such things that the kind people who attended on her could not help laughing too.

XII

The holiday was not a merry one at Pokróvsk. Though the day was beautiful, the people did not go out to amuse themselves, no girls sang in the street, the factory hands who had come home from town for the day did not play on their concertinas and balalaíkas, and had no games with

the girls. Everybody sat about in corners, and
if they spoke, did so in a low voice, as if something
evil were there and could hear them.

It was not quite so bad in the daytime, but
when the twilight fell and the dogs began to
howl, and when, to make matters worse, a wind
arose and whistled down the chimneys, such fear
seized all the inhabitants of the place that those
who had tapers lit them in front of their icons.
He who happened to be alone in his cubicle went
to ask the neighbours' permission to stay the night
with them, to be less lonely ; and he whose business should have taken him into one of the out-
houses did not go, but pitilessly left the cattle
without fodder that night. And the holy water,
of which everyone kept some in a little bottle to
charm away anything evil, was all used up during
the evening.

That night many even heard something walking about with heavy steps up in the garret, and
the blacksmith saw a dragon fly straight towards
it. The children and the madwoman had been
removed from Polikéy's cubicle. Only the little
dead body lay there, and two old women sat and
watched, while a third, a pilgrim, was reading
psalms, actuated by her own zeal, not for the
sake of the baby, but in a vague way because of

all the misfortunes that had happened. The mistress had willed it so.

The pilgrim and the other two women themselves heard how, as soon as they finished reading a portion of the Psalter, the rafters above would tremble, and somebody would move. Then they would read, " May God arise," and all would be quiet again.

The joiner's wife invited a friend; and, not sleeping all night, with her aid drank up all the tea she had procured for the whole week. They, too, heard how the beams cracked above, and something like sacks tumbled down. The presence of the peasant watch men kept up the courage of the domestic serfs somewhat, or the latter would have died of fear that night. The peasants lay on some hay in the passage, and afterwards declared that they also had heard wonderful things up in the garret, though at the time they were conversing very peacefully among themselves about the recruiting, chewing crusts of bread, scratching themselves, and so filling the passage with the peculiar smell characteristic of peasants that the joiner's wife, happening to pass by, spat and called them " peasant-brood."

However that might have been, the suicide

was still dangling in the garret, and it was as if
that night the evil spirit himself had over-
shadowed the serfs' quarters with his huge wing,
showing his power, and coming closer to these
people than he had ever done before. At any
rate, they all felt so. I do not know if they were
right, and I even think they were quite mistaken.
I think that if some bold fellow had taken a
candle or a lantern that terrible evening, and,
crossing himself, or even not crossing himself,
had gone up to the garret—slowly dispelling with
the light of the candle the horror of the night
before him, lighting up the rafters, the cobweb-
covered chimney, the tippets left behind by the
joiner's wife—till he came to Polikéy, and if,
conquering his fears, he had raised the lantern to
the level of the head, he would have beheld the
familiar, spare figure : the feet standing on the
ground (the rope had stretched), the body leaning lifelessly to one side, no cross visible under the
open shirt, the head drooping on the breast ; the
kind face, with open, sightless eyes and the meek,
guilty smile ; and a severe calmness and silence
over all. Really, the joiner's wife, crouching in a
corner of her bed with dishevelled hair and
frightened eyes, and telling how she heard sacks
falling, is far more terrible and frightful than

Polikéy, though his cross is off and lies on a rafter.

" Up there "—*i.e.*, in the house of the pro-prietress—reigned the same horror as in the serfs' quarters. Her bedroom smelt of eau-de-Cologne and medicine. Dounyásha was melting yellow wax and making an ointment. What the oint-ment was for I don't know ; but it was always made when the lady was ill. And now she was so upset that she was quite unwell. An aunt had come to help Dounyásha keep her courage up, so there were four of them, including the little girl, sitting in the maid's room, and talking in a low voice.

" Who will go to get some oil ?" asked Doun-yásha.

" Nothing will induce me to go, Avdótya Nikoláyevna !" the second maid said decidedly.

" Nonsense ! You and Aksyúta go together."

" I'll run across alone. I'm not afraid of anything !" said Aksyúta, and at once became frightened.

" Well, then, go, dear ; ask Granny Anna to give you some in a tumbler, and bring it here ; don't spill any," said Dounyásha.

Aksyúta lifted her dress with one hand, and, being thereby prevented from swinging both arms, swung one of them twice as quickly across the line of her progression, and darted away. She was afraid, and felt that if she should see or hear anything, even her own living mother, she would perish with fright. She flew, with her eyes shut, along the familiar pathway.

XIII

" Is the mistress asleep or not ?" suddenly asked a deep peasant voice close to Aksyúta.

She opened her eyes, which she had kept shut, and saw a figure that appeared taller than the serfs' house. She screeched, and flew back so fast that her skirts floated behind her. With one bound she was in the porch, with another in the maids' room—where she threw herself, wildly yelling, on her bed.

Dounyásha, her aunt, and the other maid were paralyzed with fear, and before they had time to recover they heard heavy, slow, and uncertain steps in the passage and by their door.

Dounyásha rushed to her mistress, spilling the melted wax. The second maid hid among the petticoats that hung on the wall ; the aunt, a more determined character, was going to keep the door

6

to the passage closed, but it opened, and a peasant came into the room.

It was Doútlof, with his boat-like shoes. Paying no heed to the maids' fears, he looked round for an icon, and, not seeing the tiny saint's picture in the left-hand corner of the room, he crossed himself in front of a cupboard in which teacups were kept, laid his cap on the window-sill, and, thrusting his arm so deep into the bosom of his coat that it looked as if he were going to scratch under his other arm, he pulled out a letter with five brown seals, stamped with an anchor.

Dounyásha's aunt held her hands to her heart, and with difficulty brought out the words :

" Well, you have given me a fright ! I can't bring out a wo . . . ord ! I quite thought my last moment had come !"

" Is that the way to behave ?" said the second maid, appearing from under the petticoats.

" The mistress herself is upset," said Doun-yásha, coming out of her mistress's door. " What do you mean, shoving yourself in through the maids' entrance, without leave ? . . . Just like a peasant !"

Doútlof, without apologizing, again said that he wanted to see the lady.

" She is not well," said Dounyásha.

At this moment Aksyúta burst into such improperly loud laughter that she was obliged to hide her face in the pillow on the bed, whence, in spite of Dounyásha's and the aunt's threats, for a long time she could not lift it without going off again, as if something were bursting inside her pink print bosom and rosy cheeks. To her it seemed so funny that everybody should have taken fright, that she again hid her head in the pillows, and, as if in convulsions, scraped the floor with her shoe, and jerked her whole body.

Doútlof stopped and looked at her attentively, as if to ascertain what was happening to her, but turned away again without having made out what it was all about, and continued :

" You see, it's just this—it's a most important matter," he said. " You just go and say that a peasant has found a letter with money."

" What money ?"

Dounyásha, before going to give the information, read the address and questioned Doútlof about when and how he had found this money which Polikéy ought to have brought back from town. Having heard all the particulars, and pushed the little errand-girl—who was still convulsed with laughter—out into the hall, Dounyásha went to her mistress ; but, to Doútlof's surprise, the mistress would not see him, and did not say anything intelligible to Dounyásha.

" I know nothing, and don't wish to know anything !" the lady had said. " What peasant ? What money ? . . . I can't and won't see anyone ! He must leave me in peace."

" What am I to do ?" said Doútlof, turning the envelope over ; " it's not a small sum. What is written on it ?" he asked Dounyásha, who again read the address to him.

Doútlof seemed in doubt. He was still hoping that perhaps the money was not the mistress's, and that the address had not been read out correctly to him. But Dounyásha confirmed it, and he put the envelope back into his bosom with a sigh, and was about to go.

" I suppose I shall have to hand it over to the police," he said.

" Wait a bit ! I'll try again," said Dounyásha, stopping him, after having attentively followed the disappearance of the envelope into the bosom of the peasant's coat. " Let me have the letter."

Doútlof took it out again, but did not at once put it into Dounyásha's outstretched hand.

" Say that Doútlof found it—Semyón. . . ."

" Well, let's have it !"

" I was thinking it was just nothing—only a letter ; but a soldier read out to me that there was money inside. . . ."

" Well, then, let's have it."

" I dared not even go home first to . . ." Doútlof continued, still not parting with the precious envelope. " Inform the lady of it."

Dounyásha took it from him and went again to her mistress.

" O my God ! Dounyásha, don't speak to me of that money !" said the lady in a reproachful tone. " Only to remember that little infant. . . ."

" The peasant does not know to whom you desire it to be given, madam," Dounyásha again said.

The lady opened the envelope, shuddering at the sight of the money, and became thoughtful.

" Dreadful money ! How much evil it causes !" she said.

" It is Doútlof, madam. Will you give orders for him to go, or will you please come out and see him—and is it all there—the money ?" asked Dounyásha.

" I don't want this money. It is horrible money ! . . . What it has done ! . . . Tell him he may take it if he likes," said the lady suddenly, groping for Dounyásha's hand. " Yes, yes, yes !" she repeated to the astonished Dounyásha ; " let him take it altogether, and do what he likes with it."

" Fifteen hundred roubles," remarked Dounyásha, smiling as if at a child.

" Let him take it all !" the lady repeated impatiently. " Why, don't you understand me ? It is unlucky money. . . . Never talk to me about it ! Let the peasant who found it take it. Go ! . . . Well, go along !"

Dounyásha went out into the maids' room.

" All there ?" asked Doútlof.

" Why, you'd better count it yourself," said Dounyásha, handing him the envelope. " The orders are to give it to you."

Doútlof put his cap under his arm, and, stooping down, began to count.

" Have you got a counting-frame ?"*

Doútlof had an idea that the lady was stupid and could not count, and that that was why she ordered him to do it.

" You can count it at home—it's yours . . . the money !" Dounyásha said crossly. " ' I

* The abacus, with wires and beads to count on, is still much used in Russia.

don't want to see it,' she says ; ' give it to him who brought it.' "

Doútlof, without unbending, stared at Doun-yásha.

Dounyásha's aunt clasped her hands together.

" O holy Mother ! What happiness the Lord has sent him ! O holy Mother !"

The second maid did not believe it.

" You don't mean it, Avdótya Nikoláyevna ; you're joking !"

" Joking, indeed ! She's ordered me to give it to the peasant. . . . Come, take your money and go !" said Dounyásha, without hiding her vexation. " Sorrow to one, joy to another !"

" It's not a joke . . . fifteen hundred roubles !" said the aunt.

" It's even more," stated Dounyásha. " Well ! You'll have to offer a ten-copeck candle to Saint Nicholas," she added, with a sneer. "What! Can't you come to your senses ? If at least it had come to a poor man ! . . . He has got plenty of his own."

Doútlof at last grasped that it was not a joke, and began gathering together the notes he had spread out to count, and putting them back into the envelope. But his hands trembled, and he

kept glancing at the maids to convince himself
that it was not a joke.

"See ! He can't come to his senses, he's so
glad," said Dounyásha, implying that she de-
spised both the peasant and the money. " Come,
I'll put it in for you."

She was going to take it, but Doútlof would not
let her. He crumpled the notes together, pushed
them in farther, and took his cap.

" Glad ?"

" I hardly know what to say ! It's just . . ."

He did not finish, but waved his hand, smiled,
and went out, almost crying.

The mistress rang.

" Well, have you given it ?"

" I have."

" Well, was he very glad ?"

" He was just like a madman."

" Ah ! call him. I want to ask him how he
found it. Call him in here ; I can't come out."

Dounyásha ran out and found the peasant in
the passage. He was still bareheaded, and had
drawn out his purse, and was stooping untying
its strings, while he held the money between his
teeth. Perhaps he imagined that as long as the
money was not in his purse it was not his. When
Dounyásha called him he grew frightened.

" What is it, Avdótya . . . Avdótya Nikoláyevna ? Does she wish to take it back ? Couldn't
you say a word for me ? . . . Now, really, and
I'd bring you some nice honey."

" Indeed ! Much you ever brought !"

The door opened again, and the peasant was
brought in to the lady. He did not feel very
cheerful. " Oh dear, she'll want it back !" he
thought on his way through the rooms, for some
reason lifting his feet as if he were walking through
tall grass, and trying not to stamp with his bark
shoes. He could make nothing of his surround-
ings. Passing by a mirror, he saw some kind of
flowers and a peasant with bark shoes, lifting his
legs high, a painted gentleman with an eyeglass,
some kind of green tub, and something white. . . .
There, now ! The something white began to
speak. It was the lady. He did not understand
anything, but only stared. He did not know
where he was, and saw everything as in a
mist.

" Is that you, Doútlof ?"

" Yes, lady. . . . Just as it was, so I left it . . .
never touched . . ." he said. " I was not glad
. . . as before God ! How I've tired out my
horse ! . . ."

" Well, it's your luck !" she remarked contemptuously, though with a kindly smile. "Take it—take it for yourself."

He only stared.

"I am glad you got it. God grant that it may be of use. . . . Well, are you glad?"

"How could I help being glad? I'm so glad, lady—so glad! I will always pray for you! . . . So glad, that . . . Thank Heaven that our mistress is alive! That's all I've done."

"How did you find it?"

"Well, I mean, we are always able to do our best for our lady, quite honourably, and not anyhow. . . ."

"He is getting quite muddled, madam," said Dounyásha.

"I had been taking my nephew, the recruit, and as I was coming back along the road I found it. Polikéy must have dropped it."

"Well, then, go—go, friend! I am glad!"

"So glad, lady . . ." said the peasant. Then he remembered that he had not thanked her properly, and did not know how to behave. The lady and Dounyásha smiled, and then he again began stepping as if he were walking in very high grass, and could hardly refrain from running, so fearful was he that he might be stopped and the money taken from him.

XIV

When he had got out into the fresh air, Doútlof stepped aside from the road under the lime-trees, and even undid his girdle to get at his purse more easily, and began putting away the money. His lips were moving, stretching and drawing to-gether again—though he uttered no sound. Having put away his money and fastened his girdle, he crossed himself, and went staggering along the road as though he were drunk, so full was he of the thoughts that came rushing into his mind.

Suddenly he saw the figure of a man coming towards him. He shouted. It was Efím, with a cudgel in his hand, guarding the serfs' house.

"Ah, Daddy Semyón!" said Efím joyfully, drawing nearer (Efím felt it uncanny to be alone). "Have you got the recruits off, daddy?"

"We have. What are you after?"

"Why, I've been put here to guard Polikéy that's hanged."

"And where is he?"

"Up there, hanging in the garret, so they say," answered Efím, pointing through the darkness to the roof of the serfs' house.

Doútlof looked in the direction in which the

cudgel pointed, and, though he could see nothing, he puckered his face, screwed up his eyes, and shook his head.

" The police-officer has come," said Efím. " He'll be taken down at once. Isn't it horrible in the night, daddy ? Nothing would make me go up at night, even if they ordered me to. If Egór Miháylovitch were to kill me outright I'd not go. . . ."

" The sin . . . oh, the sin of it !" Doútlof kept repeating, evidently for form's sake, and not even thinking what he was saying. He was about to continue his way, but the voice of Egór Miháylovitch stopped him.

" Hi ! watchman ! Come here !" shouted Egór Miháylovitch from the porch of the office.

Efím answered.

" And what other peasant was standing with you just now ?"

" Doútlof."

" Ah ! and you too, Semyón ! Come along !"

Having drawn near, Doútlof, by the light of a lantern which the coachman was carrying, recognized Egór Miháylovitch and a short man with a cockade on his cap, dressed in a long uniform overcoat. This was the police-officer.

" Here, this old man will also come with us,"

said Egór Miháylovitch on seeing him. The old
man felt a bit uncomfortable, but it could not be
helped.

" And you, Efím—you're a young lad ! Run
up into the garret where he's hanged himself, and
put the ladder straight for his Honour to mount."

Efím, whom nothing could have induced to
approach the serfs' house, now ran towards it,
clattering with his bark shoes as if they were
clogs.

The police-officer struck a light and lit a pipe.
He lived about a mile and a half off, and having
been cruelly reprimanded for drunkenness by his
superior, was in a zealous mood. Having arrived
at ten o'clock in the evening, he wished to examine the body at once. Egór Miháylovitch
asked Doútlof how he came to be there. On the
way, Doútlof told the steward about the money
he had found, and what the lady had done, and
said he had come to ask Egór Miháylovitch's permission. . . . To Doútlof's horror, the steward
demanded the envelope from him, and examined
it. The police-officer even took the envelope in
his hand, and asked curtly and dryly for the particulars.

" Oh dear, the money is lost !" thought Doútlof, and began justifying himself.

But the police-officer handed the money back to him.

" What a piece of luck for the clodhopper !" he said.

" It comes handy," said Egór Miháylovitch. " He's just been taking his nephew to be conscripted, and now he'll buy him out."

" Ah !" said the policeman, and went on in front.

" Will you buy him off—Elijah, I mean ?" asked Egór Miháylovitch.

" How am I to buy him off ? Will there be money enough ? And perhaps it's not the right time. . . ."

" Well, you know best," said the steward, and they both followed the police-officer. They approached the serfs' house, where the smelly watchmen stood waiting with a lantern in the passage. Doútlof followed them. The watchmen looked guilty : perhaps because of the smell they were spreading ; for they had done nothing wrong. All were silent.

" Where ?" asked the police-officer.

" Here," said Egór Miháylovitch in a whisper. " Efím," he added, " you're a young lad . . . go on in front with the lantern."

Efím had already put a plank straight on the

top of the step-ladder, and seemed to have lost
all fear. Taking two or three steps at a time, he
was climbing up with a cheerful look, only turning round to light the way for the police-officer.
The officer was followed by Egór Miháylovitch.
When they had disappeared above, Doútlof, with
one foot on the bottom step, sighed and stopped.
Two or three minutes passed. The footsteps in
the garret were no longer heard; evidently they
had reached the body.

" Daddy, they want you," Efím called through
the opening.

Doútlof began going up. The light of the
lantern showed only the upper part of the bodies
of the police-officer and of Egór Miháylovitch beyond the rafters. Beyond them again someone else
was standing, with his back turned towards them.

This was Polikéy.

Doútlof climbed over a rafter and stopped,
crossing himself.

" Turn him round, lads !" said the police-
officer.

No one stirred.

" Efím, you're a young lad ! . . ." said Egór
Miháylovitch.

The young lad stepped across a rafter, turned
Polikéy round, and stood beside him, looking with

a most cheerful face now at Polikéy, now at the official, as a showman exhibiting an Albino or Julia Pastrána looks at the audience, ready to do anything they may wish.

" Turn him round again."

Polikéy was turned round, his arms slightly swinging, and his feet dragging on the ground.

" Catch hold, and take him down."

" Shall we chop the rope through, your Honour ?" asked Egór Miháylovitch. " Hand us a chopper, lads !"

The watchmen and Doútlof had to be told twice before they would set to ; but the young lad handled Polikéy as he would have handled a sheep's carcass. At last the rope was chopped through, and the body taken down and covered up. The police-officer remarked that the doctor would come next day ; and dismissed the people.

XV

Doútlof went homeward, still moving his lips. At first he had an uncanny feeling, but it passed as he drew nearer home, and joy gradually penetrated his heart. In the village he heard songs and drunken voices. Doútlof never drank, and this time too he went straight home.

It was late when he entered his hut. His old woman was asleep. His eldest son and his grand-children were sleeping on the top of the brick oven, and the younger one in a little room out-side. Elijah's wife alone was awake, and sat on the bench, bareheaded, in a dirty, everyday smock, wailing. She did not go out to meet her uncle, but, when he entered, sobbed louder, lamenting her fate. According to the old woman, she " lamented " very fluently and well, taking into consideration the fact that at her age she could not have had much practice.

The old woman rose and got her husband's supper ready. Doútlof turned Elijah's wife away from the table, saying : " That's enough—that's enough !"

Aksínya went away, and, lying down on a bench, continued to lament. The old woman put the supper on the table, and afterwards silently cleared it away again. The old man did not speak either. When he had said grace, he hiccoughed, washed his hands, took the counting-frame from a nail in the wall, and went into the little room outside. There he and his old woman spoke in whispers for a little while ; and then, after she had gone away, he began counting on the frame, making the beads click. At last he

banged the lid of the chest standing there, and
went down into the cellar under the room. For
a long time he went on bustling about between
the room and the cellar.

When he re-entered, it was dark in the hut.
The wooden splint that served for a candle had
gone out. His old woman, quiet and silent in the
daytime, had rolled herself up on the sleeping-
bunk, and filled the hut with her snoring. Elijah's
noisy wife was also asleep, breathing quietly.
She lay on the bench, dressed just as she had
been, and with nothing under her head to serve
as a pillow. Doútlof began to pray, then looked
at Elijah's wife, shook his head, put out the light,
hiccoughed again, and climbed up on to the oven,
where he lay down beside his little grandson. He
threw his plaited bark shoes down from the oven
in the dark and lay on his back, looking up at the
rafter—hardly discernible above the oven-top just
over his head—and listening to the sounds of the
cockroaches crawling along the walls, of sighs,
snoring, rubbing of foot against foot, and the
noise made by the cattle outside. It was a long
time before he could sleep. The moon rose. It
grew lighter in the hut. He could see Aksínya
in her corner, and something he could not make
out : was it a coat his son had forgotten, or a

tub the women had put there, or someone standing ?

Perhaps he was drowsing, perhaps not ; anyhow, he began to peer into the darkness. Evidently that evil spirit which had led Polikéy to commit his awful deed, and whose nearness was felt that night by all the domestic serfs, had stretched out his wing and reached across the village to the house in which lay the money that he had used to ruin Polikéy. At least, Doútlof felt his presence, and was ill at ease. He could neither sleep nor get up. After noticing the something he could not make out, he remembered Elijah, with his hands bound, and Aksínya's face and her rhythmical lamentations ; and he recalled Polikéy, with his swinging hands.

Suddenly it seemed to the old man that someone passed by the window. "Who was that ? Could it be the village Elder coming so early to call a Meeting ?" thought he. "How did he open the door ?" thought the old man, hearing a step in the passage. "Had the old woman forgotten to draw the bolt when she went out into the passage ?" The dog began to howl in the yard, and *he* came stepping along the passage —so the old man related afterwards—as if *he* were trying to find the door, then passed on, and began groping along the wall, stumbled over a tub and made it clatter, and again began groping, as if feeling for the latch. Now he pulled the handle and entered, in the shape of a man. Doútlof knew it was *he*. He wished to cross himself, but could not. *He* approached the table, which was covered with a cloth, and, pulling off the cloth, threw it on the floor, and began climbing on to the oven. The old man knew that *he* had taken the shape of Polikéy. *He* was showing his teeth, and his hands were swinging about. *He* climbed up, tumbled on to the old man's chest, and began to strangle him.

"The money's mine!" muttered Polikéy.

"Let go! Never again!" Semyón tried to say, but could not.

Polikéy was pressing down on him with the weight of a mountain. Doútlof knew that if he said a prayer *he* would leave him alone, and knew which prayer he ought to say, but could not get it out.

His grandson, sleeping beside him, uttered a shrill scream, and began to cry. His grandfather had pressed him against the wall. The child's cry loosened the old man's lips.

"May the Lord arise! . . ." he said.

He pressed less hard.

" . . . and burst asunder . . ." spluttered Doútlof. *He* got off the oven. Doútlof heard him
strike the floor with both feet. Doútlof went on
repeating in turn all the prayers he knew. *He*
went towards the door, passed the table, and
banged the door so that the whole hut shook.
However, everybody but the grandfather and
grandson continued to sleep. The grandfather,
trembling all over, muttered prayers, while the
grandson was crying himself to sleep and clinging
to his grandfather. All became quiet once more.
The old man lay still. A cock crowed behind the
wall close to Doútlof's ear. He heard the hens
stirring, and a cockerel unsuccessfully trying to
crow in answer to the old cock. Something
moved over the old man's legs. It was the cat ;
she jumped from the oven on to the floor with her
soft paws, and stood mewing by the door. The
old man rose and opened the window. It was
dark and muddy in the street. Crossing himself,
he went out barefoot into the yard to the horses.
One could see that *he* had been there too. The
mare standing under the shed beside a tub of
chaff had got her foot into the cord of her halter,
had spilt the chaff, and now, holding up her foot,
turned her head and waited for her master. Her
foal had tumbled behind a heap of manure. The

old man raised it to its feet, disentangled the mare's foot and fed her, and went back to the hut. The old woman got up and lit the splint.

" Wake the lads ! I'm going to town !" And, taking a wax taper from the icon, Doútlof lit it and went down with it into the cellar. Not only in his hut, but in all the neighbouring houses the lights were burning when he came up again. The young fellows were up and preparing to start. The women were coming and going with pails of milk. Ignát was harnessing the horse to one cart, and the second son was greasing the wheels of another. The young wife was no longer sobbing. She had made herself neat, and had bound a shawl over her head, and now sat waiting till it would be time to go to town to say good-bye to her husband.

The old man appeared particularly stern. He did not say a word to anyone, put on his best coat, tied his girdle round him, and with all Polikéy's money in the bosom of his coat, went to Egór Miháylovitch.

" Mind you don't dawdle," he called to his son, who was turning the wheels on the raised and newly greased axle. " I'll be back in a minute ; see that everything is ready."

The steward had only just got up, and was

drinking tea. He, too, was preparing to go to town, to hand over the recruits.

" What is it ?" he asked.

" Egór Miháylovitch, I want to buy the lad off. Do be so good ! You said t'other day that you knew one in the town that was willing . . . Explain it to me, how to do it ; we are ignorant people."

" Why, have you reconsidered it ?"

" I have, Egór Miháylovitch. I'm so sorry . . . a brother's child, after all, whatever he may be. . . . I'm sorry for him ! . . . It's the cause of much sin, money is. Do be so good and explain it to me !" he said, bowing low.

Egór Miháylovitch, as was his wont on such occasions, stood for a long time thoughtfully smacking his lips ; and, having considered the matter, wrote two notes, and explained what was to be done in town, and how to do it.

When Doútlof got home, the young wife had already set off with Ignát. The fat grey mare stood ready harnessed in the gateway. Doútlof broke a twig out of the hedge, and, lapping his coat over, got into the cart and whipped up the horse. He made the mare run so fast that her fat sides gradually shrank, and Doútlof did not look at her, so as not to awaken any feeling of pity in himself. He was tormented by the thought that he might come too late for the recruiting, that Elijah would go as a soldier, and the devil's money would remain on his hands.

I will not describe all Doútlof's proceedings that morning. I will only say that he was specially lucky. The man to whom Egór Miháylovitch had given him a note had a volunteer quite ready, who had already spent twenty-three roubles, and had already been passed by the Court. His master wanted four hundred roubles for him, and a buyer in the town had for the last three weeks been offering him three hundred. Doútlof settled the matter in a couple of words.

" Will you take three and a quarter hundred ?" he said, holding out his hand, but with a look that showed that he was prepared to give more. The master held back his hand, and went on asking four hundred.

" You won't take a quarter ?" Doútlof said, catching hold with his left hand of the man's right, and preparing to smack it with his own right hand. " You won't take it ? Well, Heaven help you !" he said suddenly, smacking the master's hand with the full swing of his other arm, and turning away with his whole body.

" Evidently it must come to that . . . take three

and a half hundred ! Get the receipt ready, and
bring the fellow along. And now, here are two
ten-rouble notes on account. Is it enough ?"

And Doútlof unfastened his girdle and got out
the money.

The master, though he did not draw away his
hand, yet did not seem quite to agree, and, not
accepting the deposit money, went on stipulating
that Doútlof should wet the bargain and stand
treat to the volunteer.

" Don't you commit a sin," Doútlof kept repeating, as he held out the money. " We shall
all have to die some day," he went on, in such a
gentle, persuasive and assured tone that the
master said :

" Well, all right !"

Doútlof smacked his hand again, and began
praying for God's blessing. They woke up the
volunteer, who was still sleeping after yesterday's
carouse, thought fit to examine him, and went
with him to the offices of the Administration.

The volunteer was merry. He demanded rum
to get screwed on, for which Doútlof gave him
some money, and only when they came into the
vestibule did he become abashed. For a long
time they stood in the anteroom, the old master
in his full blue cloak, and the volunteer in a short

fur coat, his eyebrows raised and his eyes staring. For a long time they whispered, asked to be allowed to go somewhere or other, looked for somebody or other, and for some reason took off their caps and bowed to every scrivener they met, and meditatively listened to the decisions read out by a scrivener whom the master knew. All hope of getting the business done that day began to vanish, and the volunteer was growing more cheerful and unconstrained again, when Doútlof saw Egór Miháylovitch, seized on him at once, and began to beg and bow to him.

Egór Miháylovitch helped him so efficiently that by about three o'clock, to his great dissatisfaction and surprise, the volunteer was taken into the hall and placed for examination, and amid general merriment (in which for some reason everybody joined, from the watchmen to the President), he was undressed, dressed again, shaved, and let out at the door ; and five minutes later Doútlof counted out the money, received the receipt, and, having taken leave of the volunteer and his master, went to the lodging-house where the Pokróvsk recruits were staying.

Elijah and his young wife were sitting in a corner of the kitchen ; and as soon as the old man came in they stopped talking, and looked at him with a resigned expression, but not with good-will. As was his wont, the old man said a prayer; and he then unfastened his girdle, got out a paper, and called into the room his eldest son Ignát and Elijah's mother, who was in the yard.

"Don't go sinning, Elijah," he said, coming up to his nephew. "The other day you said a word to me. . . . Don't I care about you? I remember how my brother left you to me. If it were in my power, would I have let you go? God has sent me luck, and I am not grudging it you. . . . Here it is, the paper"; and he put the receipt on the table, and carefully smoothed it out with his stiff, crooked fingers.

All the Pokróvsk peasants, the inn-keeper's men, and even some outsiders, came in from the yard. All guessed what was happening, and no one interrupted the old man's solemn speech.

"Here it is, the paper! I've given four hundred roubles for it. Don't reproach your uncle."

Elijah rose, but remained silent, not knowing what to say. His lips quivered with emotion. His old mother came up, and was about to throw herself, sobbing, on his neck; but the old man motioned her away slowly and authoritatively, and continued to speak.

"You said a word to me yesterday," the old

man again repeated. " You stabbed me to the heart with that word, as with a knife ! Your dying father left you to me, and you have been as my own son to me, and if I have offended you in any way—well, we all live in sin ! Is it not so, Orthodox Christians ?" he said, turning to the peasants who stood round. " Here is your own mother and your young missis . . . and here is the receipt. . . . Never mind the money, and forgive me, for Christ's sake !"

And, turning up the skirts of his coat, he slowly sank on his knees and bowed down before Elijah and his wife. The young people tried in vain to stop him, but not till his forehead had touched the ground did he get up. Then, after giving his skirts a shake, he sat down.

Elijah's mother and wife sobbed with joy, and words of approbation were heard among the crowd. " That's according to truth, that's the godly way," said one. " What's money ? You can't buy a fellow for money," said another. " What joy !" said a third ; " in a word, he's a just man !" Only the recruits said nothing, and went softly out into the yard.

Two hours later Doútlof's two carts were passing out of the suburb of the town. In the first, to which was harnessed the grey mare, her

sides fallen in and her neck moist with sweat, sat
the old man and Ignát. Behind them jerked
a couple of bundles, containing a small caldron
and a string of ring-shaped cakes. In the second
cart, in which nobody held the reins, the young
wife and her mother-in-law, with shawls over their
heads, were sitting, dignified and happy. The
former held a bottle of vódka under her apron.
Elijah, very red in the face, sat all in a heap with
his back to the horse, jolting on the front of the
cart, biting into a cake and talking incessantly.
The voices, the rumbling of the cart-wheels on
the stony road, and the snorting of the horses
blent into one merry sound. The horses,
swishing their tails, increased their speed more
and more, feeling themselves on the homeward
road. The passers-by involuntarily turned round
to look at the happy family party.

At the very outskirts of the town, the Doútlofs
began to overtake a party of recruits. A group
of them were standing in a circle outside a public-
house. One of the recruits, with that unnatural
expression on his face which comes of having the
front of the head shaved, his grey cap pushed
back, was vigorously strumming on a balalaíka ;
another, bareheaded and with a bottle of vódka
in his hand, was dancing inside the circle. Ignát

got down to tighten the traces. All the Doútlofs looked with curiosity, approval, and merriment at the dancer. The recruit seemed not to see anyone, but felt that the numbers of the admiring public had increased, and this added to his strength and agility. He danced briskly. His brows were frowning, his ruddy face was set, and his lips were fixed in a grin that had long since lost all meaning. It seemed as if all the strength of his soul was concentrated on placing one foot as quickly as possible after the other, now on the heel, now on the toe. Sometimes he stopped suddenly and winked to the player, who began playing still more briskly, strumming on all the strings, and even knocking the case with his knuckles. The recruit would stop, but even when he stood motionless he still seemed to be dancing. Then he began slowly jerking his shoulders, and suddenly twirling round leaped in the air, and descending crouched down, throwing out first one leg and then the other. The little boys laughed, the women shook their heads, the men smiled approvingly. An old sergeant stood quietly by, with a look that seemed to say : " You think it wonderful, but we have long been familiar with it." The balalaíka-player appeared tired ; he looked lazily round, struck a

false chord, and suddenly knocked on the case
with his knuckles, and the dance came to an
end.

" Eh, Alyósha," he said to the dancer, pointing
at Doútlof, " there's your godfather !"

" Where ?   You, my dearest friend !" shouted
Alyósha, the very recruit whom Doútlof had
bought ; and staggering forward on his weary
legs and holding the bottle of vódka above his
head, he moved towards the cart.

" Míshka, a glass !" he cried to the player.
" Master . . . you're my dearest friend.   What a
pleasure, really !" he shouted, drooping his tipsy
head over the cart, and he began to treat the
men and women to vódka.   The men drank, but
the women refused.

" My own friends, what could I present you
with ?" exclaimed Alyósha, embracing the old
woman.

A woman selling eatables was standing among
the crowd.   Alyósha noticed her, seized her tray,
and poured its contents into the cart.

" I'll pay, no fear, you devil !" he howled tear-
fully, pulling a purse from his pocket and throwing it to Míshka.   He stood leaning with his
elbows on the cart, and looking with moist eyes
at those who sat inside.

" Which is the mother . . . you ?" he asked.
" I'll make an offering to you too."

He stood thinking for a moment, then he put
his hand in his pocket and drew out a new folded
handkerchief, hurriedly took off a towel which
was tied round his waist under his coat, and also
a red scarf he was wearing round his neck ; and,
crumpling them all together, shoved them into
the old woman's lap.

" There ! I'm sacrificing them to you," he
said in a voice that was growing softer and softer.

" What for ? . . . Thank you, sonny ! Just
see what a simple lad it is !" said the old woman,
addressing Doútlof, who had come up to their
cart.

Alyósha was quite quiet, quite stupefied, and
looked as if he were falling asleep. He drooped
his head lower and lower.

" It's for you I am going, for you I am perishing . . ." he muttered ; " that's why I am giving
you presents."

" I dare say he, too, has a mother," said someone in the crowd. " What a simple fellow ! It's
awful !"

Alyósha lifted his head. " I have a mother,"
said he ; " I have a father. All have given me
up. . . . Listen to me, you old one," he went on,

taking the old woman's hand. " I have offered
you gifts. . . . Listen to me for Christ's sake !
Go to the village of Vódnoye, ask for the old
woman Níkonovna—the same is my own mother,
see ? Say to this same old woman, this Níkonovna, the third hut from the end, by a new
well . . . Tell her that Alyósha—your son, you
see. . . . Eh ! you musician ! strike up !" he
shouted.

And, muttering something, he immediately
began dancing again, and hurled the bottle with
the remaining vódka to the ground.

Ignát got into the cart, and was about to start.

" Good-bye ! May God give you . . ." said
the old woman, wrapping her cloak closer round
her.

Alyósha suddenly stopped.

" Drive to the devil !" he shouted, clenching
his fists. " May your mother ! . . ."

" O Lord !" said Elijah's mother, crossing
herself.

Ignát touched the reins, and the carts rattled
on again. Alyósha the recruit stood in the
middle of the road with clenched fists and with
a look of rage on his face, and abused the peasants
with all his might.

" What are you stopping for ? Go on, devil !

cannibal !" he cried. " You'll not escape my hand ! . . . Devil's clodhoppers !"

At these words his voice broke off, and he fell full length to the ground, just where he stood.

Soon the Doútlofs had driven out into the fields, and, looking round, could no longer see the crowd of recruits. Having gone some four miles at a walking pace, Ignát got off his father's cart, where the old man lay asleep, and walked beside Elijah.

Together they emptied the bottle they had brought from town. After a while Elijah began a song, the women joined in, and Ignát shouted merrily in tune with the song. A mail-cart drove gaily towards them and passed by at full speed. The driver called lustily to his horses as he came by the merry carts ; and the postman turned round and winked at the red-faced men and women who sat jolting inside.

1863.

II

A PRAYER

" Your Father knoweth what things ye have need of,
before ye ask Him."—MATT. vi. 8.

" No, no, no ! It can't be.   . Doctor !
Surely something can be done ?   Why do neither
of you speak ?" said a young mother, as with
long, firm steps she came out of the nursery,
where her three-year-old child, her first and
only son, lay dying of water on the brain.

Her husband and the doctor, who had been
talking together in subdued tones, became
silent. With a deep sigh the husband timidly
approached her, and tenderly stroked her dishevelled hair. The doctor stood with bowed
head, and his silence and immobility showed the
hopelessness of the case.

" What's to be done ?" said the husband.
" What's to be done, dear ? . . ."

" Ah ! Don't . . . don't !" cried she ; and
there was a note of anger or reproach in

her voice as she suddenly turned back to the nursery.

Her husband tried to stop her.

" Kitty, don't go there . . ."

She glanced at him with large, weary eyes, and, without answering, entered the nursery.

The boy lay in his nurse's arms, a white pillow under his head. His eyes were open, but he did not see with them ; and from his closed lips came bubbles of foam. The nurse sat with stern and solemn mien, looking across him, and did not move when the mother entered. Only when the latter came close to her and put her hand under the pillow to take the child, the nurse said gently :

" He is passing away !" and turned aside. But his mother, nevertheless, with a deft and practised movement, took the boy into her own arms. His long wavy hair had got tangled. She smoothed it, and looked into his face.

" No, I can't . . ." she muttered, and quickly but carefully handed him back to the nurse, and left the room.

It was the second week of the boy's illness, and all that time his mother had wavered between despair and hope. During all that time she had not slept two hours a day. Several times each day she had gone to her bedroom, and, standing before the large icon of the Saviour, in its gold-embossed covering, had prayed God to save her boy. The dark-faced Saviour held in his small dark hand a gilt book, on which was written in black enamel : " Come unto Me, all ye that labour and are heavy laden, and I will give you rest."

She prayed with all the strength of her soul before that icon. And though in the depth of her heart, even while she prayed, she felt that the mountain would not be removed, and God would not do as she willed, but as He willed, she still prayed, repeating the familiar prayers, and some that she composed herself and repeated aloud with special fervour.

Now that she knew he was dead, she felt as if something had snapped in her head and was whirling round ; and when she reached her bed-room she looked at all the things there with astonishment, as though not recognizing the place. Then she lay down on the bed, her head falling not on the pillow but on her husband's folded dressing-gown, and she lost consciousness in sleep.

In her sleep she saw her Kóstya, with his curly hair and thin white neck, healthy and merry, sitting in his little arm-chair, swinging his plump little legs, pouting his lips, and carefully seating his boy-doll on the papier-mâché horse which had lost one leg and had a hole in its back.

" What a good thing he is alive !" she thought, " and how cruel it was that he died ! Why was it ? Why should God—to whom I prayed so earnestly—let him die ? Why should God wish it ? . . . He did no harm to anyone. . . . Doesn't God know that my whole life is wrapped up in him, and that I cannot live without him? To take such an unfortunate, dear, innocent being, and torture him . . . and in answer to all my prayers, to shatter my life, and let his eyes set, and his body stretch out and grow stiff and cold ! . . ."

Again she saw him coming. Such a little fellow, passing in at such big doors, swinging his little arms as grown-up people do. And he looked and smiled. . . . " The darling ! . . . and God wants to torture and destroy *him !* Why pray to Him, if He does such horrible things ?"

Suddenly Molly, the under-nurse, began to say something very strange. The mother knew it was the girl Molly, yet it was both Molly and an angel at the same time.

" But if she is an angel, why has she no wings on her back ?" thought the mother.

She remembered, however, that someone—she did not know who, but some trustworthy person—had told her that there were angels without wings now.

And Molly, the angel, said :

" You do wrong, ma'am, to be offended with God. It is impossible for Him to grant all prayers. People often ask such things, that to please one would mean offending another. . . . Why, even now, all over Russia, people are praying—and what people ! The very highest bishops and monks, in the cathedrals and churches, over the relics of the saints . . . praying for victory over the Japanese. But is that right ? It is wrong to pray for that, and He cannot grant such prayers. . . . The Japanese also pray for victory, and there is but one Father of all. . . . Then what is He to do ? What can He do, ma'am ?" repeated Molly.

" Yes, that's true ! The old story. . . . Voltaire already said it. . . . We all know it, and all say it ; but my case is different. . . . Why can't He grant my prayer when I do not ask anything bad, but only that He should not kill my darling boy, without whom I cannot live ?"

So said the mother, and she felt his plump

little arms round her neck, and his warm little body nestling against hers.

" How good that it did not really happen ! . . ." thought she.

" But that is not all, ma'am . . ." Molly insisted, in her usual blundering way. " That is not all. Sometimes only one person asks, and yet He can't possibly do it. . . . We know that, quite well ! . . . I know it, you see, because I take His messages," said Molly, the angel, in just the same voice in which yesterday, after taking a message from her mistress to her master, she told the nurse : " I know master is at home, for I have taken him a message."

" How often have I had to report to Him," said Molly, " that someone—a young one generally—asks to be helped not to do bad deeds, not get drunk or live loosely—asks, in fact, that vice should be extracted from him as if it were a splinter !"

" How well Molly speaks !" thought her mistress.

" . . . But He cannot possibly do it, for each one must try for himself. . . . Only by trying does one get better. You yourself, ma'am, gave me a fairy-tale to read about a black hen which gave a magic hemp-seed to a boy who saved her life. As long as the seed was in his trouser-pocket, he knew all his lessons without learning them, and so this seed made him stop learning and quite lose his memory. . . . He, our Father, cannot take evil out of people ; and they should not ask Him to do it, but they should pull it out—wash it out—tear it out of themselves !"

" Where has she got all this from ?" thought her mistress, and said :

" All the same, Molly, you have not answered my question."

" Give me time, and I will answer it," said Molly. " It sometimes happens that I take a message to say that a family have been ruined by no fault of their own. They are all weeping. . . . Instead of living in good rooms, they live any-how. They even go without tea, and pray for any sort of help. . . . But, again, He cannot do what they want, for He knows what is good for them. They do not see it, but He, our Father, knows that if they lived in plenty they would be spoilt and go all to smithereens."

" That's true," thought her mistress. " But why does she speak in such an off-hand way when talking about God ? ' All to smithereens ' is not at all a proper expression ! I shall cer-tainly have to tell her of it, another time."

" But that is not my question," repeated the mother. " I ask, why . . . for what reason . . . did this God of yours want to take my boy ?"

And the mother saw her Kóstya alive, and heard his childish laugh, clear as a bell. " Why should he be taken from me ? If God can do that, He is a bad, wicked God, and I do not want Him, and do not wish to know Him."

And, strange to say, Molly was no longer at all like Molly, but was some quite other, new strange indefinite creature, and she spoke, not aloud with her lips, but in some peculiar way that went straight into the mother's heart.

" Pitiful, blind, self-confident creature !" said this being. " You see your Kóstya as he was a week ago, with firm elastic limbs and long curly hair, and his naive affectionate and sensible talk. But was he always like that ? There was a time when you were glad when he could say ' Dada ' and ' Mamma,' and knew one from the other. Before that, you were delighted when he stood up on his soft feet and toddled to a chair. Before that, you were all delighted when he crawled about the room like an animal ; and earlier yet, you were glad that he began to take notice and could hold up his hairless head, the pulsating crown of which was still soft. Still

earlier, you were glad when he began to suck,
pressing the nipple with his toothless gums.
Before that, you were glad when he, all red and
not yet separated from you, cried pitifully,
filling his lungs with air. Earlier yet, a year
before, where was he—when he did not exist ?
You all think you are standing still, and that you
and those you love ought always to remain what
you now are. But you do not really remain the
same for a single minute . . . you all flow like a
river ; and as a stone drops downwards, you are
all hastening towards death, which sooner or
later awaits every one of you. How is it you do
not understand that if, from nothing, he became
what he was, he would not have stopped, and
would not for a minute have remained as he was
when he died ? But, just as from nothing he
became a suckling, and from a suckling a child, so
from a child he would have become a schoolboy,
a youth, a young man, middle-aged, elderly, and
then old. You do not know what he would have
been had he remained alive . . . but I know !"

And suddenly the mother saw—in the private
cabinet of a restaurant, brilliantly lit by elec-
tricity (her husband had once taken her to such
a place), near a table on which were the remains
of a supper—a bloated, wrinkled, unpleasant,

would-be-young old man with turned-up moustaches. He was sitting on a soft sofa, in which he sank deep, his drunken eyes gazing with desire at a depraved, painted woman with a white bare neck, and with drunken tongue he shouted something, repeating an indecent joke several times, evidently pleased at the approving laughter of another similar pair.

" It is not true, it is not he . . . that is not my Kóstya !" exclaimed the mother in terror, looking at the horrible old man—horrible just because there was something in his glance and about his lips that reminded her of Kóstya's own peculiarities. " It is well that this is only a dream," thought she. " There is the real Kóstya . . ." and she saw her white, naked Kóstya, with his plump chest, as he sat in his bath, laughing and kicking ; and she not only saw, but felt, how he suddenly seized her arm, bared to the elbow, and kissed it and kissed it, and at last bit it—not knowing what else to do with that arm so dear to him.

" Yes, this—and not that horrid old man—is Kóstya," she said to herself. And thereupon she awoke, and came back with terror to the reality from which there was no awaking.

She went to the nursery. The nurse had

already washed and laid out Kóstya's body. He
lay on something raised; his little nose was
waxen and sharp, and sunk at the nostrils, and
his hair was smoothed back from his brow.
Around him candles were burning, and on a
small table at his head stood hyacinths—white
lilac and pink.

The nurse rose from her chair and, lifting her
brows and pouting her lips, looked at the upturned, stonily rigid face. Molly entered at the
door opposite, with her simple good-natured
face and tear-stained eyes.

" Why, she told me one should not grieve, but
she has herself been crying," thought the mother.
Then she turned her gaze to the dead. For a
moment she was startled and repelled by the
dreadful likeness the dead face bore to that of the
old man she had seen in her dream; but she drove
away that thought, and, crossing herself, touched
with her warm lips the small cold waxen forehead. Then she kissed the crossed rigid little
hands; and suddenly the scent of the hyacinths
told her, as it were afresh, that he was gone and
would return no more; and she was stifled by
sobs, and again kissed him on the forehead, and
wept for the first time. She wept, but not with
despair; her tears were resigned and tender.

She suffered, but no longer rebelled or complained ; and she knew that what had happened had to be, and was therefore good.

" It is a sin to weep, dear lady," said the nurse ; and, going up to the little corpse, with a folded handkerchief she wiped away the tears the mother had left on Kóstya's waxen forehead.

" Tears will sadden his little soul ! It is well with him now. . . . He is a sinless angel. Had he lived, who knows what might have become of him ?"

" Yes, yes ! . . . But, still, it hurts, it hurts !" said the mother.

1905.

III

KORNÉY VASÍLYEF

I

Kornéy Vasílyef was fifty-four when he had last visited his village. There was no grey to be seen in his thick curly hair, and his black beard was only a little grizzly at the cheek-bones. His face was smooth and ruddy, the nape of his neck broad and firm, and his whole strong body padded with fat as a result of town life and good fare.

He had finished army service twenty years ago, and had returned to the village with a little money. He first began shopkeeping, and then took to cattle-dealing. He went to Tcherkásy, in the province of Kief, for his " goods "—that is, cattle—and drove them to Moscow.

In his iron-roofed brick house in the village of Gáyi lived his old mother, his wife and two children (a girl and a boy), and also his orphan nephew—a dumb lad of fifteen—and a labourer.

Kornéy had married twice. His first wife was a weak, sickly woman who died without having any children; and he, a middle-aged widower, had married a strong, handsome girl, the daughter of a poor widow from a neighbouring village. His children were by this second wife.

Kornéy had sold his last lot of cattle so profitably in Moscow that he had about three thousand roubles [£300]; and having learnt from a fellow-countryman that near their village a ruined landowner's forest was for sale at a bargain, he thought he would go in for the timber trade also. He knew the business, for before serving in the army he had been assistant clerk to a timber merchant, and had managed a wood.

At the railway-station nearest to Gáyi, Kornéy met a fellow-villager, "one-eyed Kouzmá." Kouzmá came from Gáyi with his pair of poor shaggy horses to meet every train, seeking for fares. Kouzmá was poor, and therefore disliked all rich folk, and especially Kornéy, of whom he spoke contemptuously.

Kornéy, in his cloth coat and sheepskin, came out of the station and stood in the porch, portmanteau in hand, a portly figure, puffing and looking about him. It was a calm, grey, slightly frosty morning.

"What, haven't you got a fare, Daddy Kouzmá?" he asked. "Will you take me?"

" Yes, for a rouble I will."

" Seventy copecks is plenty."

" There, now ! He's stuffed his own paunch, but wants to squeeze thirty copecks out of a poor man !"

" Well, all right, then . . . drive up !" said Kornéy.

And, placing his portmanteau and bundle in the small sledge, he sat down, filling the whole of the back seat. Kouzmá remained on the box in front.

" All right, drive on."

They drove across the ruts near the station and reached the smooth highroad.

" Well, and how go things in the village— with you, I mean ?" asked Kornéy.

" Why, not up to much."

" How's that ? . . . And is my old mother still alive ?"

" The old woman's alive. She was at church t'other day. She's alive, and so is your missis. . . . She's right enough. She's taken a new labourer."

And Kouzmá laughed in a queer way, as it seemed to Kornéy.

" A labourer ? Why, what's become of Peter ?"

" Peter fell ill. She's taken Justin from Ká- menka—from her own village, you see."

" Dear me !" said Kornéy.

When Kornéy was courting Martha, there had been some talk among the womenfolk about this Justin.

" Ah, yes, Kornéy Vasílyef !" Kouzmá went on ; " the women have got quite out of hand nowadays."

" No doubt about it," muttered Kornéy. " But your grey horse has grown old," he added, wishing to change the subject.

" I am not young myself. He matches his master," answered Kouzmá, touching up the shaggy, bow-legged gelding with his whip.

Halfway to the village was an inn where Kornéy, having told Kouzmá to stop, went in. Kouzmá led his horses to an empty manger, and stood pulling the harness straight, without looking Kornéy's way, but expecting to be called in to have a drink.

" Come in, won't you, Daddy Kouzmá ?" said Kornéy, coming out into the porch. " Come in and have a glass."

" I don't mind if I do," answered Kouzmá, pretending not to be in a hurry.

Kornéy ordered a bottle of vódka, and offered some to Kouzmá. Kouzmá, who had eaten nothing since morning, soon got intoxicated ; and immediately sidling up to Kornéy, began to repeat in a whisper what was being said in the village—namely, that Kornéy's wife, Martha, had taken on her former lover as labourer, and was now living with him.

"What's it to me ? . . . But I'm sorry for you," said tipsy Kouzmá. "It's not nice, and people are laughing. One sees she's not afraid of sinning. ' But,' thinks I, ' just you wait a bit ! Presently your man will come back !' . . . That's how it is, brother Kornéy."

Kornéy listened in silence to Kouzmá's words, and his thick eyebrows descended lower and lower over his sparkling jet-black eyes.

"Are you going to water your horses ?" was all he said, when the bottle was empty. "No ? Then let's get on !"

He paid the landlord, and went out.

It was dusk before he reached home. The first person he met there was this same Justin, about whom he had not been able to help thinking all the way home. Kornéy said, "How do you do ?" to this thin, pale-faced, bustling Justin, but then shook his head doubtfully.

"That old hound, Kouzmá, has been lying," thought he. "But who knows ? Anyhow, I'll find out all about it."

Kouzmá stood beside the horses, winking towards Justin with his one eye.

" So you are living here ?" Kornéy inquired.

" Why not ? One must work somewhere," Justin replied.

" Is our room heated ?"

" Why, of course ! Martha Matvéyevna is there," answered Justin.

Kornéy went up the steps of the porch. Hearing his voice, Martha came out into the passage, and, seeing her husband, she flushed, and greeted him hurriedly and with special tenderness.

" Mother and I had almost given up waiting for you," she said, following him into the room.

" Well, and how have you been getting on without me ?"

" We go on in the same old way," she answered ; and snatching up her two-year-old daughter, who was pulling at her skirts and asking for milk, she went with large firm strides back into the passage.

Kornéy's mother (whose black eyes resembled her son's) entered the room, dragging her feet in their thick felt boots.

" Glad you've come to see us," said she, nodding her shaking head.

Kornéy told his mother what business had

brought him, and remembering Kouzmá, went
out to pay him.

Hardly had he opened the door into the passage, when, right in front of him by the door
leading into the yard, he saw Martha and Justin.
They were standing close together, and she was
speaking to him. Seeing Kornéy, Justin scuttled
into the yard, and Martha went up to the
samovár standing there, and began adjusting the
roaring chimney put on to make it draw.

Kornéy passed silently behind her stooping
back, and, taking his portmanteau and bundle out
of the sledge, asked Kouzmá into the house to
drink tea. Before tea, Kornéy gave his family
the presents he had brought from Moscow : for
his mother, a woollen shawl; for his boy Fédka,
a picture-book ; for his dumb nephew, a waistcoat ; and for his wife, print for a dress.

At the tea-table Kornéy sat sullen and silent,
only now and then smiling reluctantly at the
dumb lad, who amused everybody by his delight
at the new waistcoat. He did not know what to
do for joy. He put it away, unfolded it again,
put it on, and smilingly kissed his hand, looking
gratefully at Kornéy.

After tea and supper, Kornéy went at once to
the part of the hut where he slept with Martha

and their little daughter. Martha remained in the larger half of the hut to clear away the tea-things. Kornéy sat by himself at the table, leant his head on his hand, and waited. Rising anger towards his wife stirred within him. He took down a counting-frame from a nail in the wall, drew his notebook from his pocket, and to divert his thoughts began making up his accounts. He sat reckoning, looking towards the door, and listening to the voices in the other half of the house.

Several times he heard the door go, and steps in the passage, but not hers. At last he heard her step and a pull at the door, which yielded. She entered, rosy and handsome, with a red ker-chief on her head, carrying her little girl in her arms.

" You must be tired out after your journey," said she, smiling, as if not noticing his sullen looks.

Kornéy glanced at her, and, without replying, again began calculating, though he had nothing more to count.

" It's getting late," she said, and, setting down the child, she went behind the partition. He could hear her making the bed and putting her little daughter to sleep.

"People are laughing," thought Kornéy, re-calling Kouzmá's words. "But just you wait a bit!" And, breathing hard, he rose slowly, put the stump of his pencil into his waistcoat pocket, hung the counting-frame on its nail, and went to the door of the partition. She was standing facing the icons and praying. He stopped and waited. She crossed herself many times, bowed down, and whispered her prayers. It seemed to him that she had already finished all her prayers, and was repeating them over and over again. But at last she bowed down to the ground, got up, whispered a few more words of prayer, and turned towards him.

"Agatha is already asleep," said she, pointing to the little girl, and smilingly sat down on the creaking bed.

"Has Justin been here long?" said Kornéy, entering.

With a quiet movement she threw one of her heavy plaits over her bosom, and with deft fingers began unplaiting it. She looked straight at him and her eyes laughed.

"Justin? . . . Oh, I don't know. Two or three weeks. . . ."

"You are living with him?" brought out Kornéy.

She let the plait drop from her hands, but immediately caught up her thick hard hair again, and began plaiting it.

" What won't people invent ?   I . . . live with Justin !"   She pronounced the name " Justin " with a peculiar ringing intonation.   " What an idea !   Who said so ?"

" Tell me, is it true or not ?" said Kornéy, clenching his powerful fists in his pockets.

" What's the use of talking such rubbish ? . . . Shall I help you off with your boots ?"

" I am asking you a question . . ." he insisted.

" Dear me ! . . .   What a treasure !   Fancy Justin proving a temptation to me !" she said. " Who's been telling you lies ?"

" What were you saying to him in the passage ?"

" What was I saying ?   Why, that the tub wanted a new hoop. . . .   But what are you bothering me for ?"

" I command you : tell me the truth ! . . . or I'll kill you, you dirty slut !"

And he seized her by the plait.   She pulled it out of his hand, and her face contracted with pain.

" Beating's all I've ever had from you !   What good have I had of you ? . . .   A life like mine's enough to drive one to anything !"

" . . . To what ?" uttered he, approaching her.

" What have you pulled half my plait out for ?
There . . . it's coming out by handfuls ! . . . What
are you bothering for ?   And it's true ! . . ."

She did not finish.   He seized her by the arm,
pulled her off the bed, and began beating her
head, her sides, and her breast.   The more he
beat her, the fiercer grew his anger.   She
screamed, defended herself, and tried to get away ;
but he would not let her go.   The little girl woke
up and rushed to her mother.

" Mammy !" she cried.

Kornéy seized the child's arm, tore her from
her mother, and threw her into a corner as though
she were a kitten.   The child gave a yell, and
for some seconds became silent.

" Murderer ! . . .   You've killed the child !"
shouted Martha, and tried to get to her daughter.
But he caught her again, and struck her breast
so that she fell back and also became silent.   But
the little girl was again screaming, desperately
and unceasingly.

His old mother, without her kerchief, her grey
hair all in disorder and her head shaking, tottered
into the room, and, without looking either at
Kornéy or at Martha, went to her grand-
daughter, who was weeping desperately, and
lifted her up.

Kornéy stood breathing heavily, looking about as if he had just woke up and did not know where he was or who was with him.

Martha raised her head, and groaning, wiped some blood from her face with her sleeve.

" Hateful brute !" said she. " Yes, I am living with Justin, and have lived with him ! . . . There, now, kill me outright ! . . . And Agatha is not your daughter, but his ! . . ." and she quickly covered her face with her elbow, expecting a blow.

But Kornéy seemed not to understand anything, and only sniffed and looked about him.

" See what you've done to the girl ! You've put her arm out," said his mother, showing him the dislocated, helpless arm of the girl, who did not cease screaming. Kornéy turned away, and silently went out into the passage and into the porch.

Outside it was still frosty and dull. Hoarfrost fell on his burning cheeks and forehead. He sat on the step and ate handfuls of snow, gathering it from the handrail. From indoors came Martha's groans and the girl's piteous cries. Then the door into the passage opened, and he heard his mother leave the bedroom with the child and go through the passage into the other half of the house. He rose and returned to the bedroom. The half-turned-down lamp on the table gave a dim light. From behind the partition came Martha's groans, which grew louder when he entered.

In silence he put on his outdoor things, drew his portmanteau from under the bench, packed it, and tied it up with a cord.

" Why have you killed me ?   What for ? . . . What have I done to you ?" said Martha in a doleful voice.

Kornéy, without replying, lifted his portmanteau and carried it to the door.

" Felon ! . . .   Brigand ! . . . Just you wait ! Do you think there's no law for the likes of you ?" said she bitterly, and in quite a different voice.

Kornéy, without answering, pushed the door with his foot, and slammed it so violently that the walls shook.

Going into the other part of the house, Kornéy roused the dumb lad and told him to harness the horse. The lad, half awake, looked at his uncle with astonishment, questioningly, and scratched his head with both hands. At last, understanding what was wanted of him, he jumped up, drew on his high felt boots and torn coat, took a lantern, and went to the door.

It was already quite light when Kornéy, in the small sledge, drove out of the gateway with the dumb lad, and went back along the same road he had driven over in the evening with Kouzmá.

He reached the station five minutes before the train started. The dumb lad saw how he bought his ticket, carried his portmanteau, and took his place in the carriage, and how he nodded to him, and the train moved out of sight.

Besides the blows on her face, Martha had two smashed ribs and a broken head. But the strong, healthy young woman recovered within six months, so that no trace of her injuries remained.

The girl, however, was maimed for life. Two bones were broken in her arm, and it remained twisted.

Of Kornéy, from the time he went away nothing more had been heard, and no one knew whether he was alive or dead.

II

Seventeen years had passed. It was late in autumn. The sun did not rise high all day, and twilight descended before four in the afternoon.

The communal herd of Andréyevo village was returning from pasture. The herdsman, hired for the summer, had completed his engagement and gone away, so that the village women and children were taking turns to drive the cattle.

The herd had just left the fields of oat-stubble where they had been grazing ; and, continually bleating and lowing, moved slowly towards the village, along the black, unmetalled road indented all over with cloven hoof-prints and cut by deep ruts. Ahead of the herd walked a tall, grey-bearded old man, with curly grey hair and black eyebrows. His patched coat was black with moisture, and he had a leather wallet on his bent back. He walked heavily, dragging his feet in their clumsy, down - trodden, foreign - looking boots, and leaned on his oak staff at every other step. When the herd overtook him, he stopped and leant on his staff. The young woman who was driving the herd, her skirt tucked up, a piece of sacking over her head, and a man's boots on her feet, kept running with quick steps from side to side of the road, urging on the sheep and pigs that lagged behind. When she overtook the old man she stopped, looked at him, and said in her sweet young voice :

" How do you do, daddy ?"*

* Not meant as a claim to relationship, but merely as a friendly form of greeting.

" How d'ye do, my dear ?" replied the old man.

" You'll be wanting a night's lodging, eh ?"

" Yes, it seems so . . . I'm tired," said the old man in a hoarse voice.

" Don't go and ask the Elder, daddy, but come straight to us," she said kindly. " Ours is the third hut from the end. My mother-in-law lets pilgrims in free."

" The third hut ? That's Zinóvyef's ?" said the old man, moving his black eyebrows expressively.

" Ah, do you know it ?"

" I've been here before."

" Fédya, what are you gaping at there ? The lame one has stopped behind !" cried the young woman, pointing to a sheep limping on three legs and lagging behind the herd ; and, swinging her switch with her right hand, she pulled the sacking well over her head, catching it from underneath with her left hand in a peculiar way as she ran back to drive the lame black sheep on.

The old man was Kornéy ; the young woman was Agatha, whose arm he had broken seventeen years before. She had married into a well-to-do peasant family at Andréyevo, three miles from Gáyi.

*   *   *   *   *

From a strong prosperous proud man, Kornéy Vasílyef had become what he now was : an old beggar possessing nothing but the shabby clothes on his back, and two shirts and a soldier's passport which he carried in his wallet. This change had come about so gradually that he could not tell when it began nor how it happened. The one thing he knew, and was sure of, was that his wicked wife had been the cause of all his misfortunes. It was strange and painful to him to remember what he had once been; and when he did remember it, he also remembered and hated her whom he considered to be the cause of all the evil he had suffered these seventeen years.

After that night when he beat his wife, he had gone to the landowner whose wood was for sale, but he was unsuccessful : the wood had already been sold. So he returned to Moscow, and there took to drink. Before this he used to drink at times, but now he drank for a fortnight on end. When he came to himself he went south to buy cattle. His purchase proved unlucky, and he lost money. He went again, but lost a second time ; and in a year his three thousand roubles had dwindled to twenty-five, and he was obliged to work for an employer instead of being his own master. From that time onwards he drank more and more often. For a year he lived as assistant to a cattle-dealer, but had a drinking bout while on the road, and the dealer dismissed him. Then, through a friend, he got a place as shopman at a wine and spirit dealer's, but did not stay there long, either, for his accounts got wrong, and he was dismissed. Shame and anger prevented his returning home.

"Let them live without me! Maybe the boy is not mine, either," thought he.

Matters went from bad to worse. He could not live without drink, and could no longer get employment as a clerk, but only as a cattle-drover. At last no one would take him even for that.

The more wretched his own plight became, the more he blamed her, and the fiercer his anger against her burnt within him.

The last time Kornéy found a place as a drover was with a stranger. The cattle fell ill. It was not Kornéy's fault, but his master got angry, and dismissed both him and the clerk over him. As he could get no employment, Kornéy resolved to go on pilgrimage.

He provided himself with a pair of boots and a good wallet, took some tea and sugar, and, with eight roubles in his pocket, started for Kief. Kief did not satisfy him, and he went on to New

Athos, in the Caucasus; but, before reaching it, he fell ill with ague, and suddenly lost all his strength. He had only one rouble and seventy copecks left, and he knew no one, so he decided to return home to his son.

"That wicked wife of mine may be dead by now," thought he as he journeyed homewards; "or if she's still alive, I'll tell her everything before I die, that the wretch may know what she has done to me."

The fever-attacks came on every other day. He grew weaker and weaker, so that he could not walk more than eight or ten miles. When still a hundred and fifty miles from home, he had no money at all left, and had to beg his way in Christ's name, and to sleep where the village officials lodged him.

"Rejoice at what you have brought me to," said he, mentally addressing his wife, and from habit he clenched his feeble old fists. But there was no one to strike, and his fists had no strength left in them.

It took him a fortnight to walk those last hundred and fifty miles. Quite ill and worn out, he reached the place three miles from home, where he met Agatha, who was wrongly considered to be his daughter, and whose arm he had broken.

10

III

He did as Agatha suggested. On reaching the Zinóvyefs' house he asked leave to spend the night there. They let him in.

On entering the hut he, as usual, crossed himself before the icon, and greeted his hosts.

" You're frozen, daddy ! Get up on to the oven !" said the wrinkled cheerful old housewife, clearing away the things on the table.

Agatha's husband, a young-looking peasant, sat on a bench by the table, trimming the lamp.

" How wet you are, daddy !" said he. " Well, it can't be helped. Make haste and dry yourself !"

Kornéy took off his coat, bared his feet, hung his leg-bands up to dry near the oven, and himself climbed on to the top of it.

Agatha entered the hut, carrying a jug. She had already driven the herd home, and had attended to the cattle.

" Has an old pilgrim been here ?" asked she. " I met one, and told him to call."

" There he is," said her husband, pointing to the oven, on which sat Kornéy, rubbing his lean and hairy legs.

When tea was ready, they asked Kornéy to join them. He climbed down, and seated himself at the end of a bench. They handed him a cup of tea and a piece of sugar.

The talk was about the weather and the harvest. There was no getting the corn in. The land-owner's sheaves were sprouting in the fields. As soon as one started carting them, down came the rain again. The peasants had pretty well got theirs in, but the landowner's corn was rotting like mad. And the mice in the sheaves were just dreadful !

Kornéy told of a field he had seen as he came along which was still full of sheaves.

The young housewife poured him out a fifth cup of the weak, pale yellow tea, and handed it to him.

" Never mind if it is your fifth, daddy, it will do you good," said she, when he made as if to refuse it.

" How is it your arm is not all right ?" he asked her, twitching his eyebrows, and carefully taking the full cup she handed him.

" It was broken when she was still a baby—her father wanted to kill our Agatha," said the talkative old mother-in-law.

" What was that for ?" asked Kornéy. And, looking at the young housewife's face, he sud-denly remembered Justin with his light blue eyes, and the hand in which he held his cup shook so that he spilt half the tea before he could set it on the table.

"Why, her father—who lived at Gáyi—was a man named Kornéy Vasílyef. He was well-to-do; and high and mighty with his wife. He beat her and injured the child."

Kornéy was silent, glancing, from under his continually twitching black eyebrows, first at the husband and then at Agatha.

"What did he do that for?" asked he, biting a morsel off his piece of sugar.

"Who knows? Tales of all sorts get told about us women, and we have to answer for them all," said the old woman. "They had some row about their labourer. . . . The man was a good fellow from our village. He died afterwards at their house."

"He died?" asked Kornéy, and cleared his throat.

"Died long ago. From them we took my daughter-in-law. They were well off. When the husband was alive they were the richest folk in the village."

"And what became of him?" asked Kornéy.

"He died, too, I suppose. He disappeared at the time—some fifteen years ago now."

" It must be more. Mother used to tell me she had not long weaned me when it happened."

" And don't you bear a grudge against him, because of your arm ?" began Kornéy—with a sob.

" No ! Wasn't he my father ? It's not as if some stranger had done it. . . . Have another cup, after being so cold. Shall I pour it out for you ?"

Kornéy did not reply, but burst into tears and sobs.

" What's the matter ?"

" It's nothing—nothing. May Christ reward you !"

And with trembling hands Kornéy took hold of the bunk and the post supporting it, and with his long thin legs climbed on to the oven.

" There, now !" said the old housewife to her son, making a sign in the direction of their visitor.

IV

Next day Kornéy was the first to rise. He climbed down from the top of the oven, rubbed his dried and stiffened leg-bands, painfully drew on his mud-clogged boots, and slung the wallet on to his back.

" Why, daddy, you'd better have some breakfast," said the old housewife.

" The Lord bless you ! . . .   I'll be going."

" Well, then, at least take some of yesterday's cakes with you.   I'll put them into your wallet."

Kornéy thanked her, and took his leave.

" Call in when you return.   If we are still alive . . ."

Outside everything was wrapped in dense autumn fog, but Kornéy knew the way well ; he knew every descent and ascent, every bush, and all the willows along the road, right and left— though during the last seventeen years some had been cut down and from old had become young again, while others that had been young had grown old.

The village of Gáyi was still the same, though some new houses had been built at the end, where none stood before ; and some of the wooden houses had been replaced by brick ones.   His own brick house had not changed except to grow older. The iron roof had long needed repainting, some bricks had been knocked away at one corner, and the porch leaned to one side.

As he approached the house that had been his, the gates creaked, and out came a mare with its foal, a roan gelding, and a two-year-old colt. The old roan was just like the mare Kornéy had bought at the fair the year before he left home.

"It must be the very one she was in foal with at the time. It's got just her slanting haunches, broad chest, and shaggy legs," thought he.

A black-eyed boy, wearing new bark shoes, was taking the horses to water.

"It must be Fédka's boy—my grandson—he's got just his black eyes," thought Kornéy.

The boy glanced at the old stranger and ran after the colt that was frisking in the mud. A dog as black as old Wolfey followed the boy.

"Can it be Wolfey?" thought he, and remembered that Wolfey would have been twenty by now. He came to the porch, ascended with difficulty the steps on which he had sat that night swallowing snow from the hand-rail, and opened the door leading into the passage.

"Where are you shoving to, without leave?" came a woman's voice from inside. He recognized her voice. And then she herself, a withered, sinewy, wrinkled woman, looked out of the room. Kornéy had expected to see the young and handsome Martha, who had offended him so deeply. He hated *her*, and wished to reproach her, but now this old woman appeared in her stead.

"If it's alms you want, ask at the window," she said, in a shrill, harsh voice.

"No, it's not alms," said Kornéy.

" Well, what is it you do want ?   Eh ?"

She stopped suddenly; and by her face he saw that she recognized him.

" There are plenty of the likes of you loafing about ! Go away, go away . . . in Heaven's name !"

Kornéy fell back against the wall, supporting himself with his staff, and looked intently at her. He was surprised to find that he no longer felt the anger he had nursed against her all these years, but that a mixed feeling of tenderness and languor had suddenly overcome him.

" Martha ! . . .   We shall have to die soon . . ."

" Go . . . go, in Heaven's name !" said she, rapidly and angrily.

" Is that all you have to say ?"

" I have nothing to say," she answered. " Go . . . for Heaven's sake ! Go, go ! . . . There are plenty of you ne'er-do-well devils loafing about !"

She hurriedly re - entered the room, and slammed the door.

" Why scold ?" he heard a man say ; and a dark peasant—such as Kornéy had been forty years before, only shorter and thinner, but with the same sparkling black eyes—came out, with an axe stuck in his belt.

This was that same Fédka to whom, seventeen years before, he had given a picture-book. It was he who was now reproaching his mother for showing no pity to the beggar. With him came the dumb nephew, also with an axe at his belt. He was now a grown man, wrinkled and sinewy, with a thin beard, long neck, and a determined, penetrating glance. Both men had just finished their breakfast, and were going to the woods.

" Wait a bit, daddy," said Fédka, and, turning to his dumb companion, he pointed first to the old man and then to the room, and made a movement as if cutting bread.

Fédka went into the street, and the dumb man returned to the room. Kornéy, his head hanging down, still stood in the passage, leaning against the wall and supporting himself on his staff. He felt quite weak, and could hardly check his sobs. The dumb man returned from the room with a large chunk of fresh, sweet-smelling black bread, which he gave to Kornéy. When Kornéy, having crossed himself, took the bread, the dumb man turned towards the room door, passed his hands before his face, and made as though he spat— thereby expressing his disapproval of his aunt's conduct. Suddenly he stopped dead, opened his mouth, and fixed his eyes on Kornéy as though he recognized him.   Kornéy could no longer restrain his tears ; and, wiping his eyes, nose, and grey beard on the skirt of his coat, turned away and went out into the porch.

He was overcome by a strange feeling of tenderness, elation, humility and meekness towards all men : to *her*, to his son, to everybody ; and this feeling rent his soul with pain and joy.

*   *   *   *   *

Martha looked out of the window, and breathed freely only when she saw the old man disappear behind the corner of the house.

When she was sure he had gone, she sat down at her loom and began weaving.   Some ten times she struck with the batten, but her hands would not obey her.   She stopped, and began thinking, and recalling Kornéy as she had just seen him. She knew it was he who had nearly killed her, and who, before that, had loved her ; and she was frightened at what she had just done.   She had not done right.   But how should she have treated him ?   He had not even said that he was Kornéy, and that he had come home.   And she again took the shuttle, and went on weaving till evening.

V

Kornéy with difficulty dragged himself back to Andréyevo by the evening, and again asked permission to stay the night at the Zinóvyefs'. They let him in.

" So you've not gone on, daddy ?"

" No, I felt too weak. It seems I shall have to go back. Will you let me stay the night ?"

" Oh yes ! You'll not wear out the spot you lie on. Come in and get dry."

All night Kornéy shivered with fever. Towards morning he dozed off, and when he awoke the family had all gone out to work. Only Agatha remained in the hut.

He was lying on the shelf-bed, on a dry coat the old woman had spread for him.

Agatha was taking bread out of the oven.

" My dear," he said, in a feeble voice, " come here !"

" Coming, daddy," she answered, getting out the loaves. " Want a drink ? A drop of kvas ?"

He did not answer.

When she had taken out all the loaves, she brought him a bowl of kvas. He did not turn towards her, and did not drink, but lay, face upwards, and began speaking without looking at her.

" Agatha," he said, " my time has come. I am going to die. So forgive me, for Christ's sake !"

" God will forgive you. You have done me no harm."

He was silent awhile.

" One thing more. Go to your mother, my dear. Tell her, ' The pilgrim ' . . . say, ' yesterday's pilgrim ' . . . say . . ."

He broke into sobs.

" Then have you been to my home ?"

" Yes. Say, ' Yesterday's pilgrim . . . the pilgrim ' . . . say . . ."

Again he broke off, sobbing; but at last, gathering strength, he finished :

" Say I wished to make peace," he said, and began feeling on his chest for something.

" I'll tell her . . . I'll go and tell her ! But what are you searching for ?" said Agatha.

Without answering, the old man, frowning with the effort, drew a paper from his breast with his thin, hairy hand, and gave it to her.

" Give this to him who asks for it. It's my soldier's passport. . . . God be thanked, my sins are over now !" And his face took on a triumphant expression. His brows rose, his eyes were fixed on the ceiling, and he was quiet.

" A candle . . ." he uttered, without moving his lips. Agatha understood, took a half-burnt wax taper from before the icon, lit it, and put it in his hand. He held it up with his thumb.

Agatha went to put the passport in her box, and when she returned to him the candle was falling from his hand, his fixed eyes no longer saw anything, and his chest was motionless.

Agatha crossed herself, put out the candle, took a clean towel, and covered his face with it.

* * * * *

All that night Martha had not slept, but kept thinking about Kornéy. In the morning she put on her coat, threw a shawl over her head, and went to find out where the old man had gone to. She soon learnt that he was at Andréyevo. Martha took a stick from the fence and went towards Andréyevo. The farther she went, the more frightened she grew.

" I'll make it up with him, and we'll take him home. Let the sin be ended. Let him at least die at home, with his son near him," thought she.

When Martha approached her daughter's house, she saw a large crowd collected there. Some had entered the passage, others stood outside the windows. It had already got about that the well-known, rich Kornéy Vasílyef, who had been so much talked of in the district twenty years before, had died, a poor wanderer, in his daughter's house. The house was full of people. The women whispered to one another, sighed and moaned.

When Martha entered, they made room for her to pass, and under the icons she saw the body—already washed, laid out, and covered with a piece of linen. At its side Philip Kanónitch (who had had some education) was chanting the words of a psalm in Slavonic, in a voice like a deacon's.

Neither to forgive nor to ask forgiveness was any longer possible; and from the stern, beautiful old face of Kornéy she could not tell whether he had forgiven her or not.

1905.

IV

It was June, and the weather was hot and still. In the forest the foliage was thick, sappy and green, and only rarely did a yellow leaf fall here and there from a birch or a lime-tree. The wild-rose bushes were covered with sweet blossoms ; and the forest glades were a mass of honey-scented clover. The thick, tall and waving rye was growing darker, and its grain was swelling fast. In the low-lying land the corncrakes called to one another ; in the rye and the oat field quails croaked and cried noisily ; in the forests at rare intervals the nightingales sang a few notes and then were again silent. The heat was dry and scorching, and the dust lay an inch thick on the road, or rose in dense clouds, blown now to left and now to right by a stray gentle breeze.

The peasants were working to finish their buildings or were carting manure. The hungry cattle were out on the dry fallow land, awaiting

159

the aftermath in the hayfields. The cows and calves were lowing, and, with uplifted hooked tails, abandoned their shady resting-places to scamper away from the herdsmen. By the road-side and on the banks, lads were pasturing horses; women were carrying sacks of grass out of the woods; young maidens and little girls, hurrying after one another, crept between the bushes where the trees were felled, picking strawberries to sell to the gentlefolk who had come to the country for the summer.

These summer inhabitants of ornamented, architecturally pretentious bungalows, strolled with open sunshades, in light, clean, costly clothes, along sand-strewn paths; or sat in the shade of trees and arbours, by decorated tables, and, overpowered by the heat, drank tea or sipped cooling drinks.

Before the splendid bungalow of Nicholas Semyónovitch, with its tower, veranda, little balconies and galleries (everything about it fresh, new, and clean), stood a troika - calèche with three horses, that had brought a Petersburg gentleman from the town six miles off.

This gentleman—a well-known and active Liberal member of every Committee—was on every Council, and signed every petition and

every address—cunningly framed to appear faithfully loyal, but really very radical. He had come
from the town (in which, as an extremely busy
man, he was staying only twenty-four hours) to
see the old friend and playmate of his childhood,
who was almost his adherent.

They disagreed only on the best way of putting
their Constitutional principles into practice ; and
as to that but slightly. The Petersburger was
more of a European—even with a slight leaning
towards Socialism—and in receipt of a very large
salary from the different posts he occupied.
Nicholas Semyónovitch, on the other hand, was
a pure Russian, Orthodox, a bit of a Slavophil,
and the owner of many thousands of acres.

They had had five courses for dinner, which
was served in the garden ; but the heat made it
almost impossible to eat, so that all the work of
the cook (who received £50 a year) and of his
assistants, who had taken special trouble to prepare dinner for the visitor, was wasted. They
had only eaten of the iced fish-soup, and the parti-
coloured, prettily shaped ice-pudding, elaborately
ornamented with spun sugar and biscuits. Besides the visitor, there had been present at dinner
a Liberal doctor, the children's tutor—a desperately Socialistic, Revolutionary student (but

whom Nicholas Semyónovitch was able to keep within bounds)—Nicholas Semyónovitch's wife, Marie, and their three children ; the youngest of whom came only to dessert.

There had been a slight strain during dinner, because Marie, a very nervous woman, was anxious about the derangement of Gógo's stomach (as is the custom among well-bred people, the name " Gógo " was given to their youngest son, Nicholas), and also because, as soon as a political subject was started by Nicholas Semyónovitch and the visitors, the desperate student—in his eagerness to show that he was not afraid of ex-pressing his opinions to anyone—broke into the conversation. Then the visitor would cease talking, and Nicholas Semyónovitch would try to soothe the student.

They had dined at seven ; and after dinner the friends sat on the veranda, refreshing themselves by sipping iced *narzán** with white wine, and conversing.

Their difference of opinion first showed itself on the question of elections : as to whether direct or secondary representation was better—and the discussion was growing heated when they were called to tea in the dining-room, which was care-

* A mineral water from the Caucasus.

fully protected from the flies by nets. The conversation at tea was general, and directed to Marie, who could take no interest in it because her thoughts were absorbed by some symptoms of the derangement of Gógo's digestive organs. They were talking about pictures, and Marie maintained that in decadent art there was a certain *je ne sais quoi :* which could not be denied. She was at that moment not thinking in the least about decadent art, but only repeating what she had often said before. As for the visitor, he did not care about it at all, but he had heard what was being said against decadence, and repeated it so naturally that no one could have guessed that neither decadence nor non-decadence concerned him in the least ; and Nicholas Semyónovitch, looking at his wife, felt that she was dissatisfied about something, and that some unpleasantness might be expected—and, besides, it was very dull listening to what she was saying. He thought he must have heard it at least a hundred times.

Rich bronze lamps were lit inside the room, and lanterns outside. The children had been put to bed ; Gógo having first been subjected to medical treatment.

The visitor, with Nicholas Semyónovitch and the doctor, went out on to the veranda. The footman brought candles with glass globes, and more *narzán*, and about midnight they started at last a real, animated conversation as to the best means of government to be adopted at the present, most critical, time for Russia. They all smoked and talked unceasingly.

Outside the gate clanked the bells on the harness of the horses, which had not been fed, and the old driver, sitting inside the calèche, alternately yawned and snored. He had worked for one master twenty years ; and with the exception of three to five roubles a month, which he drank, he had sent all his money home to his brother, who worked their land in the village. When the cocks began to crow to one another from bungalow to bungalow (especially one from a neighbouring yard, who had a very loud shrill voice) the driver began to wonder whether they had forgotten him, and got down and went inside the gate. He saw his fare sitting, eating and talking. He became alarmed, and went to look for the footman. He found him in his livery, sitting asleep in the ante-room. The driver woke him up. The footman, formerly a serf, kept his large family out of his wages (it was a good place : he got £20 a year wages, and sometimes another £10 in tips) ; he had five girls and two boys. He jumped up, pulled himself together with a shake, and went to tell the gentleman that the driver was getting uneasy and asking to be dismissed.

When the footman entered, the discussion was at its height. The doctor also was taking part in it.

" I cannot admit that the Russian people . . ." the visitor was saying, " ought to develop on different lines. Before all things liberty is wanted —political liberty—that liberty . . . as all know well, is the greatest liberty . . . without infringing the rights of others."

He felt that he was getting a little mixed, and that that was not the right way to put it ; but he could not quite remember how it should be put.

" That is so," answered Nicholas Semyóno-vitch, anxious to express his own thought, with which he was particularly pleased, and not listening to the visitor—" that is so, but it must be reached by other means—not by a majority of votes, but by common consent. Look at the *Mir*, how it arrives at its decisions !"

" Oh, that *Mir* !"

" It cannot be denied," said the doctor, " that the Slavonic nations have an outlook of their own. Take, for instance, the Polish right of veto. I don't maintain that it is a better way . . ."

" One moment . . . I will finish what I was going to say," began Nicholas Semyónovitch. " The Russian people have special characteristics. These characteristics . . ."

But here Iván, the liveried, sleepy-eyed footman, interrupted him.

" The driver is getting uneasy," he said.

" Please tell him " (the Petersburg visitor always spoke politely to footmen, and prided himself on doing so) " that I shall soon be going, and will pay for the extra time."

" Yes, sir."

The footman went away, and Nicholas Semyónovitch was able to finish expressing his view. But both the visitor and the doctor had heard him express it a score of times (or, at any rate, they thought so), and began disproving it, especially the visitor, who quoted instances from history. He knew history very thoroughly.

The doctor sided with the visitor, admired his erudition, and was glad of the opportunity of becoming acquainted with him.

While they were engrossed in their subject the dawn appeared behind the wood on the opposite side of the road, and the birds woke up, but the arguers still kept on smoking and talking, talking and smoking, and the conversation might have

gone on still longer, if a maidservant had not
appeared at the door.

This servant was an orphan, who had had to
take service to earn her living. She had first
gone into a tradesman's house, where one of his
assistants seduced her, and she had had a child.
The child died, and she entered the house of an
official whose son—a gymnasium student—gave
her no peace ; and now she was under-housemaid
in Nicholas Semyónovitch's family, and considered
herself fortunate because she was not pursued by
her master's lust, and had her wages paid regularly.
She came to say that her mistress wanted the
doctor and Nicholas Semyónovitch.

" Oh dear ! . . ." thought Nicholas Semyónovitch, " something must be wrong with Gógo."

" What's the matter ?" he asked.

" Nicholas   Nikoláyevitch   seems   unwell."
Nicholas Nikoláyevitch—that was little Gógo,
who had overeaten himself, and was now suffering
from diarrhœa.

" And it's high time for me to be going," said
the visitor. " Just look how light it is . . . how
long we have been sitting here !" He smiled (as
if approving of himself and his collocutors for
having talked so much and so long) and took his
leave.

Iván had to run about on his weary legs, searching for the visitor's hat and umbrella, which the latter had himself left in the most unlikely places. Iván hoped to get a tip ; but the visitor—always generous, and quite ready to give him a rouble—being carried away by the discussion, clean forgot him, and remembered only when well on his way that he had not tipped the footman. " Ah well," he thought, " it cannot be helped now."

The driver mounted the box and gathered up the reins, and, sitting sideways, touched up the horses. The bells clanked, and the Petersburg gentleman, rocked on the soft springs of the calèche, drove away, his thoughts full of the narrowness of his friend's view.

Nicholas Semyónovitch, who had not gone to his wife at once, was thinking the same about his friend. " The shallow narrowness of these Petersburgers is awful, and they can't get out of it," he thought. He shrank from going to his wife, because he did not expect anything good from the interview at that moment. It was all on account of some strawberries. In the morning Nicholas Semyónovitch had bought, without even bargaining, two platefuls of not very ripe wild strawberries which some peasant boys were selling. His children came running and asking for some, and began eating them straight from the boys' plates. Marie had not yet come down. When she came and heard that Gógo, whose stomach was already out of order, had been given strawberries, she became extremely angry. She reproached her husband, and he reproached her ; so that they had some very unpleasant words— almost a quarrel.

Towards evening some unsatisfactory symptoms really showed themselves, but Nicholas Semyónovitch thought that after that everything would be all right. However, the fact that the doctor was called proved that things had taken a bad turn.

When he did go in, he found his wife in the nursery, dressed in a favourite bright-coloured silk dressing-gown, about which, however, she was not thinking at that moment, and holding a guttering candle for the doctor, who, with his pince-nez on his nose and a very attentive expression on his face, was carefully making an examination. " Yes," she said meaningly, " it is all on account of those confounded strawberries."

" What of the strawberries ?" Nicholas Semyónovitch asked timidly.

" What of the strawberries ? . . . It's you that

fed him on them, and here am I, not having a wink of sleep all night . . . and the child will die !"

" Oh, come, he won't die," said the doctor, with a smile. " Just a small dose of bismuth, and careful diet. . . . Let's give him some now."

" He's asleep," she said.

" Oh, then, it's better not to disturb him. I'll call in again to-morrow."

" Please do !"

The doctor went away, and the husband, left alone with his wife, was long unable to soothe her. It was broad daylight before he fell asleep.

Early that morning, in the neighbouring village, the lads were returning with the horses they had pastured all night. Some of them had only the one they rode ; others were leading a second horse as well, while the colts and two-year-olds ran free behind.

Taráska Resounóf, a lad of twelve in a sheep-skin coat, with a cap on his head but barefooted, seated on a piebald mare and leading a gelding by a cord, outdistanced all the others and trotted up the hill to the village. A well-fed piebald colt ran, kicking up its legs (which looked as if they had white stockings on) to right and left.

Taráska rode up to his hut, tied the horses to the gate, and entered the passage.

" Hullo, you there . . . oversleeping yourselves !" he cried to his sisters and brother, who were sleeping on some sacking in the passage.

Their mother, who had also slept there, was already up and milking the cow.

Little Ólga jumped up, smoothing down with both hands her tangled flaxen hair. But Fédka, who lay beside her, continued to lie with his head hidden in a sheepskin coat, and only rubbed with a rough little heel the shapely childish foot that peeped from under the coat.

The previous evening the children had arranged to go strawberry-picking, and Taráska had promised to call his sisters and little brother as soon as he came back with the horses. He had kept his promise. In the night, sitting under a bush, he had felt extremely sleepy, but now he was wide awake, and decided not to lie down at all, but to go strawberry-picking with the girls. His mother gave him a mug of milk and cut him a chunk of bread, and he sat down on the high bench by the table to eat his breakfast. Then, dressed only in a pair of trousers and a shirt, he hurried along the road, leaving the prints of his bare feet in the dust—which already bore a number of smaller and larger footprints, distinctly showing the imprint of the little toes. Far ahead he could see the girls, like red and white specks against the dark green of the forest. In the evening they had prepared a little jug and a mug to put the berries in ; and this morning, after crossing themselves once or twice before the icon, they had run out without breakfast, and without even taking a bit of bread with them. Taráska caught them up near the big forest, just as they turned off the road.

The bushes, and even the lower branches of the trees, were covered with dew. The girls' little bare feet at first grew cold, and then began to glow, as they stepped now on the soft grass and now on the rough earth. The strawberries grew chiefly where the trees had been felled. The girls first went to the part where the trees had been cut the year before and the young shoots had only just begun to grow : where between the sappy little bushes were patches of long grass, amid which the rosy-white strawberries—with here and there a red one—hid and ripened. The little girls, bent nearly double, picked the berries one by one with their small brown fingers, putting the worst in their mouths and the best ones into the mugs.

" Ólga dear, come here !   Here's an awful lot !"

" Nonsense ! . . . Hullo !" they called to each other when they got behind the bushes.

Taráska went farther, beyond the hollow, where the trees had been felled two years before, and where the new growth, especially the hazels and maples, was already taller than a man. The grass there was thicker and more juicy, and the berries, protected by the grass, grew juicier and larger.

" Groúsha !"

" Eh ?"

" Supposing a wolf came ?"

" Well, what about a wolf ? What do you frighten one for ? . . . I'm not afraid, I'm not !" declared Groúsha ; and absent-mindedly, her thoughts wandering to the wolf, she put berry after berry—and some of the very finest—into her mouth instead of into the mug.

" See ! our Taráska has gone beyond the ravine ! . . . Taráska, hullo ! . . ."

" Here !" answered Taráska across the ravine. " You come too !"

" Yes, let us ; there are more berries there !" And the girls clambered down into the hollow, holding on to the bushes and along the little crevices, and up again on the other side. And here they chanced at once on a spot lying in the full glare of the sunlight, covered with fine grass and sprinkled thick with strawberries ; and straightway they set to work with hands and mouths, silently and without pausing. Suddenly something rustled through the stillness, and with a terrible noise (as it seemed to them) rattled and clattered among the grass and bushes.

Groúsha fell down with a fright, upsetting the already half-filled jug. " Mammy !" she whimpered, and began to cry.

" A hare, a hare ! . . . Taráska, a hare ! . . . There he is !" shouted little Ólga, pointing to the grey-brown back that gleamed through the bushes. " What's the matter with you ?" she said to Groúsha, when the hare had disappeared.

" I thought it was a wolf," answered Groúsha, and her terror and tears of despair changed instantly to loud laughter.

" There's a stupid !"

" I was dreadfully frightened," said Groúsha, with peals of ringing laughter. They picked up the berries and went on. The sun was now up, and threw bright flecks and shadows on the green, and glittered in the dew that lay everywhere, and that had now saturated the girls' clothes up to their waists.

The girls had nearly reached the end of the

wood, having gone on and on in the hope that the farther they went the more strawberries there would be, and now the shrill voices of girls and women who had come out later to pick berries, resounded from every side. The girls' mug and jug were nearly full when they came across Aunty Akoulína, who had also come strawberrying. Behind her a little fat-bellied, bareheaded boy, with nothing on but a shirt, waddled along on thick bandy legs.

"Here, he hangs on to me," said Aunty Akoulína to the girls, taking the boy up in her arms, "and I have no one to leave him with."

"And we have just scared a hare; such a clatter he made . . . dreadful!"

"Dear me!" said Akoulína, and put the boy down again. Having exchanged these words, the girls parted from Akoulína and went on with their work.

"Suppose we rest a bit now," said little Ólga, sitting down in the shade of a hazel-bush. "I'm tired! . . . Oh dear, we've not brought any bread! It would be nice to eat a bit now!"

"I'd like some, too."

"What's Aunty Akoulína shouting about? Hear? . . . Hullo, Aunty Akoulína!"

"Ólga dear . . . eh!"

" What ?"

" Have you got my boy there ?"

" No !"

The bushes rustled, and Akoulína appeared on the opposite side of a hollow, with her skirt tucked up to her knees and a basket on her arm.

" Haven't you seen my boy ?"

" No."

" Here's a nice business ! . . .   Míshka !"

" Míshka ! . . ."

No one answered.

" What a bother ! He'll get lost ! . . . He'll wander off into the big forest."

Ólga jumped up and went with Groúsha to look for him one way, and Akoulína another, unceasingly calling with their ringing voices ; but no one answered.

" I'm tired !" Groúsha kept saying, as she lagged behind Ólga, who did not stop shouting, going now to the left, now to the right, and looking from side to side.

Akoulína's tones of despair could be heard far off in the direction of the big forest. Ólga was about to give up the search, when, in one of the sappy bushes beside the stump of a lime-tree overgrown with young shoots, she heard the continuous angry, desperate chirping of some bird which probably had nestlings near by, and was displeased about something. The bird was evidently frightened and angry. Ólga looked round the bush, which was surrounded by a mass of tall grass with white blossoms, and there she saw something blue—unlike any kind of forest plant. She stopped and gazed at it. It was Míshka—whom the bird feared and was angry with.

Míshka lay on his fat stomach, sleeping sweetly, his head on his arms, his plump, crooked little legs stretched out.

Ólga called his mother, woke the boy, and gave him some of her strawberries. And for a long time after that, Ólga used to tell her father, mother, neighbours and everybody she met, how she had looked for and found Akoulína's boy.

The sun stood high above the forest, scorching the earth and everything on it.

" Ólga, come and bathe !" said some other girls she met. And the whole crowd of them went down, singing, to the river. Splashing, shrieking, and kicking about, the girls did not notice how a dark, lowering cloud arose, now hiding, now revealing the sun, nor how strong the flowers and birch-leaves began to smell, nor the low rumbling of thunder. They had hardly time to get dressed before the rain drenched them to the skin. With

their garments dark with wet and clinging to
them, the girls ran home, had something to eat,
and then took their father his dinner in the field
where he was earthing up potatoes with the
plough.

By the time they got home again and had
finished their dinner, their clothes were already
dry. Then they picked over their strawberries,
put them into bowls, and took them to Nicholas
Semyónovitch's house, where they were generally
well paid ; but this time the strawberries were
refused.

Marie, who exhausted by the heat sat in a
large easy-chair, holding an open sunshade, waved
her fan at the girls when she saw them, and
said :

" No, no ! We don't want any !"

But Vólya, her eldest, twelve-year-old son, who
was resting after his fatiguing work at the Classical
Gymnasium and playing croquet with some neighbours, saw the strawberries and ran up to Ólga.

" How much are they ?"

" Thirty copecks," said she.

" That's too much," he replied, because the
grown-up people spoke like that. "Wait a bit—
just step round the corner," he added, and ran to
the nurse.

Ólga and Groúsha admired the large globe mirror-ornament which stood in the garden, in which one could see tiny little houses, woods and gardens. This globe, as well as many other things, did not surprise them, because they expected to see the most wonderful things in this mysterious, and to them incomprehensible, gentlefolks' world.

Vólya came to his nurse and asked her to give him thirty copecks. Nurse said it was too much, but produced twenty from her box. Then, going round out of his way to avoid his father (who had only just got up after his weary night, and who sat smoking and reading his paper), he gave twenty copecks to the girls, and emptied the strawberries onto a plate.

When they got home, Ólga untied with her teeth the knot in her handkerchief where she had tied the twenty copecks, and gave them to her mother; who, after putting them away, went to the river to rinse her washing.

Taráska, who had been helping his father earth up the potatoes, lay fast asleep in the shade of a dark oak. His father sat by him, keeping an eye on the horse—which he had taken out of the plough, and which was now grazing near the border of his neighbour's land—for fear it might stray among the oats or into the neighbour's meadow.

In Nicholas Semyónovitch's family everything was pursuing its usual course. All was well. The three-course lunch was ready, and the flies were eating it because nobody felt inclined for food.

Nicholas Semyónovitch was pleased with the justice of his arguments, proved by what the papers said that morning. Marie was quiet because Gógo's digestion was all right again. The doctor was satisfied because his medicine had been successful ; and Vólya was contented because he had eaten a whole plateful of strawberries.

1905.

V

WHY ?

I

In the spring of 1830 Pan Jaczéwski, at his family estate of Rozánka, received a visit from Joseph Migoúrski, the only son of a deceased friend.

Jaczéwski, a patriot of the days of the second partition of Poland, was a broad-browed, broad-shouldered, broad-chested man of sixty-five, with a long white moustache on his brick-red face. As a youth he had served with Migoúrski's father under the banner of Kosciúszko ; and with all the strength of his patriotic soul he hated the " Apocalyptic Adulteress " (as he called Catherine II) and her abominable paramour, the traitor Poniatówski ; and he believed in the re-establishment of the Polish State as firmly as he believed that to-morrow's sun would rise. In 1812 he had commanded a regiment in the army of Napoleon, whom he adored. Napoleon's fall distressed him, but he did not despair of the re-establishment of the Polish kingdom, even though

in a mutilated form.   His hopes were reawakened
when Alexander I opened the Diet in Warsaw ;
but the Holy Alliance, the general reaction in
Europe, and the obstinacy of Constantine,*
deferred the realization of this cherished hope.

Since 1825 Jaczéwski had settled in the country
and lived there, never leaving Rozánka, spending
his time in farming, hunting, and reading the
papers and letters, by means of which he still
eagerly followed the political events of his native
land.   His second marriage, to a pretty but poor
gentlewoman, was not happy.   He did not love or
respect her, considered her a burden, and treated
her harshly and rudely, as if to revenge himself
for the mistake he had made in remarrying.   He
had no children by this second wife.   By his first
wife he had two daughters : Wánda, the eldest,
a stately beauty who knew the value of her good
looks, and found country life tiresome ; and a
younger one, Albína, her father's pet, a lively,
bonny little girl, with fair curly hair, and large
sparkling grey eyes set far apart like her father's.

Albína was fifteen when Joseph Migoúrski came
to stay with them.   As a student he used to visit

* Brother of Alexander I and Nicholas I.   He was
in command in Poland from 1816, and provoked the
insurrection of 1830 by his harsh military rule.

the Jaczéwskis in Vilna, where they wintered, and
paid attentions to Wánda ; but this was the first
time that he, now a full-grown and independent
man, had come to see them in the country.
Everyone at Rozánka was pleased when young
Migoúrski came. Jaczéwski was pleased because
Josy reminded him of the companion of his youth,
Migoúrski's father, and because he spoke warmly
and with the rosiest hopes of the revolutionary
movement—not in Poland alone, but also abroad,
whence he had just returned. Pani Jaczéwski, the
lady of the house, was pleased because old
Jaczéwski restrained himself in the presence
of visitors, and did not scold her for everything as he usually did. Wánda was pleased,
because she felt sure Migoúrski had come for her
sake, and intended to propose to her. She was
preparing to accept him, but (as she expressed it to
herself) meant *lui tenir la dragée haute!** and Albína
was pleased because everybody else was pleased.
Wánda was not alone in thinking that Migoúrski had
come intending to propose to her. All the household
—from old Jaczéwski to Ludwíka, the old nurse—
thought the same, although no one spoke of it.

And it was quite true. Migoúrski came with
that intention ; but after a week's stay, confused

* " To make him sit up for it."

and upset by something, he left without having proposed.   Everyone was surprised by his strange and unexpected departure, and no one but Albína understood its cause.   Albína knew that she herself was the cause.

During the whole of Migoúrski's stay in Rozánka, she had noticed that he was especially animated and bright only when with her.   He treated her as a child, joked with her and teased her ; but her feminine instinct told her that his relation to her was not that of a grown-up person to a child, but that of a man to a woman.   She could see this in the look of love and the tender smile with which he greeted her when she entered the room, and followed her when she went out.   She did not clearly explain to herself what this meant ; but these relations between them gladdened her, and she involuntarily tried to do what pleased him.   And as everything she did pleased him, all her actions in his presence were done with especial elation.   It pleased him to see her running races with a beautiful wolfhound that jumped up and licked her flushed and radiant face ; it pleased him when, on the smallest provocation, she burst into infectiously ringing peals of laughter ; it pleased him when, with her eyes still laughing, she assumed a serious expression during the priest's dull sermons. It pleased him when, with extraordinary exactitude and drollery, she imitated—now her old nurse, now a tipsy neighbour, and now Migoúrski himself—passing instantaneously from one character to another. But what pleased him most of all was her happiness, her rapturous joy of life. It was as if she had only now fully discovered the delight of living, and hastened to make the most of it. This peculiar joy of life pleased him, and it was evoked and intensified by the very fact that she knew that her joy of life delighted him. So Albína alone knew why Migoúrski, having come to propose to Wánda, left without having done so. Though she would never have ventured to tell this to anyone, and did not even acknowledge it to herself, yet in the depth of her soul she knew that he had wished to fall in love with her sister, but had fallen in love with her—Albína. She was very much surprised at this, regarding herself as quite insignificant beside the clever, well-educated, beautiful Wánda ; but she could not help knowing that it was true, and could not help being glad of it, for she herself loved Migoúrski with her whole soul : loved him as one can only love for the first time, and only once in a lifetime.

II

Towards the end of the summer the papers brought the news of the revolution in Paris. This was followed by news of preparations for an insurrection in Warsaw. Jaczéwski, with hope and fear, was expecting by every post news of the assassination of Constantine and of the commencement of a revolution. At last, in November, tidings came of the attack on the Belvedere and the flight of Constantine; and, later, news that the Diet had declared the Románof dynasty deposed from the throne of Poland; that Chlopícki had been proclaimed Dictator, and that Poland once more was free! The rebellion had not yet reached Rozánka, but all its inmates followed its progress, expecting it to come and preparing for it. Old Jaczéwski corresponded with a former acquaintance, one of the leaders of the rebellion; received mysterious Jewish agents on business relating, not to farming, but to the revolution; and was ready to join the rising when the time should come. Pani Jaczéwski concerned herself more than ever about her husband's physical comforts, and thereby, as usual, irritated him more and more. Wánda sent her diamonds to a friend in Warsaw, that the

money they fetched might go to the Revolutionary Committee. Albína was only interested in
what Migoúrski was doing. She knew, through
her father, that he had joined Dwerníczki's
forces. Migoúrski wrote twice : first, to say that
he had joined the army ; and later, in the middle
of February, he sent an enthusiastic letter about
the victory near Stóczek, where the Poles captured six Russian guns and some prisoners.

His letter ended with the words : " The Poles
are victorious and the Russians are defeated !
Hurrah !" Albína was in raptures. She examined the map, calculated where and when the
Russians would be finally beaten, and grew pale
and trembled when her father slowly opened the
packets that arrived by post. One day her stepmother, happening to enter Albína's room, found
her standing before the looking-glass, dressed in
a pair of trousers and a man's hat. Albína was
getting ready to run away from home in male
attire to join the Polish army. Her stepmother
told her father. He called his daughter to him,
and (hiding his feeling of sympathy and even ad-
miration) rebuked her sternly, demanding that
she should give up her foolish idea of taking part
in the war. " Women have other duties : to love
and comfort those who sacrifice themselves for

their country," said he. Now he had need of
her and she was his joy and solace ; and the time
would come when she would be needed by a husband. He knew how to influence her. He
hinted at his loneliness and sorrows, and she
pressed her face against him, hiding the tears
which, for all that, wetted the sleeves of his
dressing-gown ; and she promised to undertake
nothing without his consent.

III

Only those who experienced what the Poles
endured after the partition of Poland and the
subjugation of one part of it by the hated
Germans, and of another part by the even more
hated Russians, can understand the delight the
Poles felt in 1830 and 1831 when, after their previous unfortunate attempts to regain indepen-
dence, its attainment seemed again within reach.
But these hopes did not last long. The forces
were too unequal ; and once more the revolution
was crushed. Again tens of thousands of un-
reasoningly submissive Russians were driven into
Poland. Under the leadership first of Diebitsch
and then of Paskévitch—subject to the supreme
command of Nicholas I—these Russians, with-

out knowing why, saturated the ground with their own blood and with that of their brothers the Poles, whom they crushed and again placed under the power of weak, insignificant men who cared neither for the freedom nor the subjugation of Poland, but sought only to gratify their own avarice and childish vanity.

Warsaw was captured, and the separate Polish detachments were defeated. Hundreds and thousands of men were shot, flogged to death, or exiled. Among the latter was young Migoúrski. His estate was confiscated, and he himself sent as a common soldier in a line regiment, to Urálsk.

The Jaczéwskis spent the winter of 1832 in Vilna on account of the old man's health ; for after 1831 he began to suffer from heart disease. Here they received a letter from Migoúrski. He wrote from prison, saying that, hard as what he had gone through and had yet to undergo might be, he still was glad to have had an opportunity to suffer for his native land, and did not despair of the holy cause to which he had given part of his life, and for which he was prepared to give the remainder ; and that if another chance occurred to-morrow, he would again act as he had done.

Reading the letter aloud, the old man broke down at this passage, sobbed, and was long unable to continue. In the latter part of the letter, which Wánda read out, Migoúrski wrote that *whatever plans and dreams he might have had* at the time of his last visit to them (which would ever remain the brightest spot in his life), he now neither could, nor would, speak of them.

Wánda and Albína each understood these words in her own way, and they spoke to no one of how they understood them. At the end of the letter Migoúrski sent messages to everyone, and among the rest—in the playful tone he had adopted towards Albína during his visit—he addressed her too, asking her whether she still ran as swiftly, outrunning the dogs ? Did she still mimic everybody so well ? He wished the old man good health ; the mother, success in household matters ; Wánda, a worthy husband ; and Albína, the continuance of her joy of life.

IV

Old Jaczéwski's health grew worse and worse, and in 1833 the whole family went abroad. In Baden, Wánda met a rich Polish emigrant, and married him. The old man's illness progressed rapidly, and he died abroad early in 1833, in Albína's arms. He would not let his wife nurse

him, and to the last moment could not forgive her
the mistake he had made in marrying her. Pani
Jaczéwski returned to the country with Albína.

Albína's chief interest in life was Migoúrski. In
her eyes he was the greatest of heroes and martyrs,
and to him she decided to devote her life. Even
before going abroad she began to correspond with
him, at first commissioned thereto by her father,
and then on her own account. When she returned to Russia after her father's death, she continued to correspond with him, and when she
reached the age of eighteen she announced to her
stepmother that she had decided to go to Migoúrski in Urálsk, and there to marry him.

Her stepmother began to blame Migoúrski for,
as she said, selfishly wishing to improve his sad
lot by inducing a wealthy girl, whose affections
he had secured, to share his misfortunes. Albína
thereupon became angry, and told her stepmother that no one but she could ascribe such
low motives to a man who had sacrificed everything for his native land; that, on the contrary, Migoúrski had refused the help she had
offered him; but that she had irrevocably
decided to go to him and marry him, if only
he would allow her that happiness. Albína was
legally of age, and she had money : 300,000

zlóty,* a sum that an uncle had left to each of his
two nieces; so no one could interfere.

In November, 1833, Albína bade farewell to
the household (who saw her start for barbarous
Russia as though she were going to her death),
seated herself with her old and devoted nurse
Ludwíka, whom she took with her, in her father's
old carriage—newly repaired for the great journey
—and started on her long road.

V

Migoúrski did not live in barracks, but had a
lodging of his own.   Nicholas I decreed that the
exiled Polish officers should not only bear all the
hardships of rough army life, but should be made
to suffer all the degradations to which common
soldiers at that time were subjected.   But the
majority of the plain men with whom it lay to
execute these orders, disobeyed them as far as they
could.   The half-educated commander of the
battalion in which Migoúrski was placed (a man
who had risen from the ranks) understood the
position of the educated, formerly wealthy, young
man who had lost everything; and, pitying and
respecting him, made all sorts of concessions in

* Between £4,000 and £5,000.

his favour. Migoúrski could not help appreci-
ating the good-nature of this Lieutenant-Colonel,
with white whiskers on his puffy, military face;
and to repay him, he agreed to teach mathematics and French to his sons, who were preparing
to enter a military college.

Migoúrski's life in Urálsk, which had now
lasted nearly seven months, was not only monotonous, dull and wearisome, but was also hard.
Except the commander of the battalion, from
whom as much as possible he tried to keep at a
distance, his only acquaintance was an exiled Pole,
a sly, unpleasant man of little education, who
traded in fish. But the chief hardship of
Migoúrski's life lay in the fact that he found it
difficult to accustom himself to privation. After
the confiscation of his property he had no means
whatever left, and struggled on by selling what
jewellery he still possessed.

The great and only joy of his life, after his de-
portation, was his correspondence with Albína.
A sweet, poetic image of her had remained in his
mind since his visit to Rozánka, and now, in his
exile, grew more and more beautiful. In one of
her first letters to him she asked, among other
things, what he had meant in his former letter by
the words, " Whatever plans and dreams I may

have had." He replied that he could now tell her that his dream had been to call her his wife. She wrote back saying that she loved him. He answered that she should not have written that, because it was terrible to think of what might have been, but was now impossible. She replied that it was not only possible, but would surely be ! He wrote that he could not accept such a sacrifice, and that in his present circumstances it was impossible. Soon after this letter he received a money-order for 2,000 zlóty.* By the postmark on the envelope and by the writing he knew that it came from Albína, and he remembered how in one of his first letters he had jokingly described to her the pleasure he now experienced in earning all he required by giving lessons : money to buy tobacco, tea, and even books. Putting the money-order into a fresh envelope, he returned it with a letter in which he begged her not to spoil their sacred friendship with money. He wrote that he had all he required, and was perfectly happy in the knowledge that he had such a friend—and so their correspondence ended.

In November, Migoúrski was sitting at the

---

* About £30. The purchasing power of money at that time in Poland and Russia was very much greater than it now is.

Lieutenant-Colonel's teaching the latter's two boys, when he heard the approaching sound of the post-bell, and the snow creaked under the runners of a sledge, which stopped at the front-door. The children jumped up to see who had come. Migoúrski remained in the room, looking at the door, and expecting the children to return, when the Lieutenant-Colonel's wife herself entered.

"Oh, Pan ! Here are some ladies asking for you," she said. "They must be from your parts . . . they seem to be Poles."

Had anyone asked Migoúrski if he thought it possible that Albína might come to him, he would have said that it was quite out of the question ; yet at the bottom of his heart he expected her. The blood rushed to his heart now, and he ran breathless into the hall. There a fat, pock-marked woman was unwrapping a shawl from her head. Another woman was entering the door of the Lieutenant-Colonel's rooms. Hearing foot-steps behind her, she turned round. From under the hood, eyes, set far apart and full of the joy of life, beamed beneath their frozen lashes—the eyes of Albína.

He was stupefied, and did not know how to welcome her, or how to greet her.

"Josy !" she cried, giving him the name her

father called him by, and by which she thought of him herself—and she threw her arms round his neck, pressing her cold, reddened face to his, and began to laugh and cry.

Having heard who Albína was, and why she had come, the Lieutenant-Colonel's kind-hearted wife received her into her house, and kept her there till the wedding.

VI

The good-natured Lieutenant - Colonel obtained the necessary permission from the authorities. A Polish priest was procured from Órenburg. The battalion-commander's wife took the place of the bride's mother, one of Migoúrski's pupils carried the icon, and Brzozówski, the exiled Pole, acted as best man.

Strange as it may seem, Albína loved her husband passionately, but did not know him at all. She only now began to make his acquaintance. Of course, she found in the living man of flesh and blood much that was ordinary and prosaic, and had not existed in the image she had borne and nurtured in her mind. But, on the other hand, just because he was a man of flesh and blood, she found in him much that was simple and good, and had not existed in the abstract image. She had heard from friends and acquaintances of his courage in the war, and knew how bravely he had borne the loss of his property and freedom, and she had imagined him a hero always living an exalted and heroic life. In reality, with all his extraordinary physical strength and courage, he turned out to be as mild and gentle as a lamb, an artless fellow, making good-natured jokes ; his sensuous lips, surrounded by a fair moustache and small beard, showed the same childlike smile that had attracted her at Rozánka, and he carried an ever-smoking pipe, specially unpleasant to her when she was pregnant.

Migoúrski, too, only now learnt to know Albína, and in her he first learnt to know women in general. From the women he had met before his marriage he could not have known women. And what he found in Albína as a type of women in general surprised him, and might have tended to disenchant him with them, had he not felt towards Albína, as Albína, a peculiarly tender and grateful feeling. Towards Albína as a woman he entertained a tender and rather ironical condescension ; but towards Albína as Albína not only tender love, but rapture, and the sense of an irredeemable obligation for the sacrifice she had made, which had given him undeserved happiness.

The Migoúrskis were happy in their love. Directing all their power of love to one another, among strangers they felt like two people who, having lost their way in winter, are in danger of being frozen, and warm one another. The devotion of the old nurse, Ludwíka, good-naturedly grumbling, comical, always falling in love with every man she met, but slavishly and self-sacrificingly attached to her young mistress, contributed to the Migoúrskis' happiness. They were also happy in their children. A year after their marriage, a boy was born ; and eighteen months later, a girl. The boy was the very image of his mother : the same eyes, the same vivacity and grace. The girl was a healthy pretty little animal.

The Migoúrskis' misfortune was their exile from home, and especially the unpleasant humiliation of their position. Albína, in particular, suffered from this degradation. He, her Josy, her hero— that ideal man—had to draw himself up erect before every officer he met, go through manual exercises, stand sentinel, and obey every order without demur.

Then, too, the letters they received from Poland were most depressing. Almost all their nearest friends and relations were either banished

or had fled abroad after losing everything they
possessed. For themselves, the Migoúrskis had
no prospect of an improvement in their situation.
All attempts to petition for pardon, or even for
an amelioration of their lot, or for him to be
made an officer, were vain. Nicholas I held re-
views, parades and manœuvres ; went to mas-
querades and amused himself with the masks ;
rushed needlessly across Russia from Tchougoúef
to Novorossíysk, to Petersburg and to Moscow,
frightening people and using up horses ; and when
anyone was courageous enough to address him,
begging for a mitigation of the fate of any exiled
Decembrists,* or of the Poles who were suffering
for love of their native land (the very quality he
himself extolled), he expanded his chest, fixed
his leaden eyes on anything they happened to
rest on, and said : " Too soon ! Let them continue to serve . . ." as if *he* knew the right time,
and when it would cease to be too soon. And
all about him—Generals and Chamberlains and
their wives, who got their living from him—went
into raptures at the extraordinary penetration and
wisdom of this great man.

* The Decembrists attempted, by a conspiracy, to
secure Constitutional government for Russia after the
death of Alexander I, in 1825.

On the whole, however, there was more joy than pain in the Migoúrskis' lives.

They lived thus for five years. Suddenly they were overwhelmed by a terrible and unexpected sorrow. First, their little girl fell ill, and two days later their boy also. For three days he lay burning with fever, and on the fourth he died, without medical aid (no doctor was within reach). Two days later, the little girl died too.

If Albína did not drown herself in the Urál River, it was only because she could not think without terror of the state her husband would be in when he heard of her suicide. But it was hard for her to live. Formerly always active and busy, she now left all her duties to Ludwíka, and sat for hours listlessly and silently gazing at anything her eyes fell upon ; or she would start up and run into her own little room, and there—regardless of her husband's or Ludwíka's condolences—would weep softly, only shaking her head and asking them to go away and leave her alone.

When summer came, she would go to her children's grave and sit there, rending her heart with memories of what had been, and with thoughts of what might have been. She was specially tortured by the idea that the children

might have remained alive had they lived in a
town where they could have received medical
aid. " Why ? What for ?" thought she. " Josy
and I want nothing from anyone, except that he
should be allowed to live the life he was born
to, and which his grandfathers and great-grand-
fathers lived ; and that I should be allowed to
live with him and love him, and love my little
ones, and bring them up. But they must needs
come and torment him and banish him, and rob
me of what is dearer to me than all the world.
Why ? What for ?"

She put the question to men and to God, and
could not imagine the possibility of any answer.
And without an answer there was no life for her ;
and so her life came to a standstill. Their poor
existence in exile, which she with her feminine
taste and refinement had formerly known how
to adorn, now became intolerable, not only to
her but also to Migoúrski, who suffered on her
account, and did not know how to help her.

VII

At this, the most unhappy time for the
Migoúrskis, a Pole named Rosolówski arrived at
Urálsk. He had been concerned in a wide-

spread plot organized in Siberia by the exiled Polish priest Sirocínski, to raise an insurrection and escape from exile.

Rosolówski, who, like Migoúrski and thousands of others, was being punished with exile in Siberia for wishing to remain what he had been born—a Pole—had taken part in this plot and had been flogged for it ; and he was now sent as a common soldier to serve in Migoúrski's battalion. Rosolówski, who had been a teacher of mathematics, was a tall, thin, round-shouldered man, with hollow cheeks and wrinkled brows.

On the first evening after his arrival, as he sat at tea with the Migoúrskis, he naturally began to tell them, in his slow quiet bass voice, about the affair for which he had suffered so cruelly.

It was this : Sirocínski had organized a secret society all over Siberia, the aim of which was, by the aid of the Poles serving in the Cossack and line regiments, to incite the soldiers and convicts to mutiny, to get the exiles to rise, to seize the artillery at Omsk, and to liberate everybody.

"Would that have been possible ?" asked Migoúrski.

" Certainly it would . . . everything was ready," said Rosolówski, frowning gloomily. And slowly and calmly he explained the whole plan of liberation, and all the measures taken to secure success, or, in case of failure, to save the conspirators. If two scoundrels had not betrayed the plan, success was assured. According to Rosolówski, Sirocínski was a man of genius and great spiritual power. He died like a hero and a martyr. And Rosolówski, in his calm, steady deep voice, told them the details of the execution, which, by order of the Authorities, he and all who had been tried for this affair were compelled to witness.

" Two battalions of soldiers stood in two rows, forming a long passage. Every soldier held a flexible switch, of a thickness which, by regulations Imperially confirmed, allowed three of them to go into the muzzle of a musket. The first man to be led out was Doctor Szakálski. Two soldiers led him, and the men beat him with the switches on his bare back as he passed. I only saw this when he passed the place where I stood. At first I could hear only the beating of the drum, but when I heard the swishing of the sticks and the sound of the strokes on the flesh, I knew he was approaching. I saw how the soldiers dragged him along by the musket to which he was tied, and how he went shuddering and turning his head from side to side. And once, as they led him past us, I heard a Russian doctor say to

the soldiers : ' Don't hit hard ; have some pity !'
But they continued to beat him, and when he
passed me the second time, he could no longer
walk, but was simply being dragged along. It
was dreadful to see his back ; and I closed my eyes.
He fell, and was carried away. Then another
prisoner was brought out, then a third, and then
a fourth. They all sank under it, and were all
carried away, some dead, some just alive—and we
had to stand by and witness it. It lasted six
hours, from early morning till two in the afternoon. The last to be brought out was Sirocínski
himself. I had not seen him for a long time, and
should hardly have recognized him, he had aged
so. His clean-shaven face was all wrinkled and
livid. His bare body was thin and yellow, the
ribs protruded above his shrunken stomach. He
went, as they all did, shuddering at each stroke
and jerking back his head, yet he did not groan,
but loudly repeated the prayer, *Miserere mei, Deus,
secundam magnam misericordiam tuam.*

"I heard it myself," muttered Rosolówski
quickly and hoarsely ; and, shutting his mouth
firmly, he sniffed.

Ludwíka, sitting at the window, sobbed,
hiding her face in her handkerchief.

"Why do you describe it ? Beasts—beasts

that they are !" shouted Migoúrski ; and, throwing down his pipe, he sprang from his chair and
strode rapidly into his dark bedroom.

Albína sat as if petrified, her eyes fixed on a
dark corner.

VIII

On returning home after drill next day, Migoúrski was surprised and delighted to notice a great
change in his wife. She came to meet him with
a light step and beaming face as of old, and led
him into their bedroom.

" Now, Josy, listen ! . . ."

" Yes ; what is it ?"

" I have been thinking all night of what
Rosolówski told us, and I have made up my mind.
I can't live like this—I can't live here, I can't !
I'll die rather than remain here !"

" But what can we do ?"

" Run away !"

" Run away ?   How ?"

" I have thought it all out.   Listen. . . ."

And she told him the plan she had devised
during the night.   It was this : Migoúrski was to
go away one evening and leave his overcoat on
the banks of the Urál, and with it a letter saying
he was going to take his life.   It would be sup-

posed that he had drowned himself. He would be searched for, and then the fact would be notified. But in reality he would be hidden. She would hide him so that no one would find him. It would be possible to live like that for a month, say, and when all had blown over, they would escape.

At first Migoúrski thought her scheme impracticable; but towards evening, after her passionate and confident persuading, he began to agree with her. He was the more inclined to do so because the punishment for an unsuccessful attempt to desert—such punishment as Rosolówski had described—would fall on him; while success would set her free, and he knew how hard life there had become for her since the children died.

Rosolówski and Ludwíka were taken into their confidence; and after long discussions, alterations and improvements, a plan was finally adopted. Their first idea was that when Migoúrski's death should have become an accepted fact, he should run away alone and on foot. Albína would follow in a vehicle, and meet him at some appointed place. Such was the first plan. But when Rosolówski told them of all the unsuccessful attempts that had been made to escape from Siberia during the last five years (during which

time only one lucky fellow had managed to get
away alive), Albína proposed another plan. This
was that Josy should travel to Sarátof with her
and Ludwíka, hidden in their vehicle. From
Sarátof he was to go disguised along the bank of
the Vólga, on foot, to an appointed place where
he was to meet a boat Albína would hire at Sarátof.
On this they would sail down the Vólga to
Astrakhán, and cross the Caspian Sea to Persia.
This plan was approved by all, including the
expert, Rosolówski ; but there was the difficulty
of arranging, in a conveyance, a place which would
not attract the attention of the officials and yet
could conceal a man. When, after a visit to her
children's grave, Albína told Rosolówski how
hard it was for her to leave their bodies in a
strange land, he, after thinking awhile, said :

"Petition the Authorities to let you take
the children's coffins with you. They will
allow it."

"No, I don't want to. . . . I can't do that,"
said Albína.

"You only ask, that's all ! We won't really
take the coffins, but will make a box big enough
to hold them, and will put Joseph into it."

At first Albína rejected this proposal, so unpleasant was it to her to connect deceit with the

memory of her children; but when Migoúrski cheerfully approved the scheme, she agreed.

So the final plan was worked out as follows :

Migoúrski would do all that was necessary to convince the Authorities that he had drowned himself. After his death had been accepted as a fact, Albína would present a petition for leave to return home and to take her children's bodies with her—her husband being dead. When she received this permission, the graves would be made to look as if they had been opened and the coffins exhumed ; but they would be left where they were, and, instead of them, Migoúrski would get into the box. The box would be placed in a *tarantás*,* and in this way they would travel to Sarátof. At Sarátof they would take a boat, and on the boat Josy would be released from the box, and they would sail down to the Caspian Sea, and thence to Persia or Turkey and to freedom.

IX

First of all, on the pretext of sending Ludwíka back to her native land, the Migoúrskis bought a *tarantás*. Then began the construction in the

---

* A strong conveyance, with poles for springs, specially adapted for rough travelling.

tarantás of a box, in which, without suffocation, a man could lie huddled up, and which he could easily enter and leave. The three of them— Albína, Rosolówski, and Migoúrski himself— planned and arranged this box, Rosolówski's help being specially valuable, for he was a good carpenter.

The box was arranged to rest upon the poles behind the *tarantás*, and the side touching the vehicle (from which part of the back had been removed) was made to open, so that a man could lie partly in the box and partly on the bottom of the vehicle. Besides all this, air-holes were drilled in the box (which was to be covered with matting and corded round the top and sides). He could get in and out of the box through the *tarantás*, which was furnished with a seat hiding the connection.

When the *tarantás* and the box were ready, before her husband's disappearance, Albína, to prepare the Authorities, went to the Colonel and announced that her husband was suffering from melancholia, and had attempted to commit suicide, and that she was anxious about him ; and begged for leave of absence for him. Her dramatic talent came in useful here. Anxiety and fear for her husband were so naturally ex-

14

pressed that the Colonel was touched, and promised to do what he could.   After that Migoúrski
composed a letter, which was to be found in the
cuff of his overcoat on the bank of the Urál; and
on the appointed evening he went down to the
river, waited till dark, left some clothing, with
his overcoat and a letter, on the bank, and returned home secretly.

In the garret, which was fitted with a lock, a
place had been prepared for him.   In the night
Albína sent Ludwíka to the Colonel to inform
him that her husband had been absent from home
for twenty hours, and had not yet returned.
In the morning her husband's letter was brought
to her ; and, her face bathed in tears, and with an
appearance of utter despair, she took it to the
Colonel.

A week later Albína presented a petition to be
allowed to return to her home.   The grief shown
by Madame Migoúrski affected everyone who saw
her.   They all pitied the unfortunate, widowed
mother.   When she had received permission to
leave, she presented another petition : to be
allowed to disinter the bodies of her children and
to take them with her.

The Authorities were surprised at this senti-
mentality, but gave this permission also.

The evening after she had received this second permission, Rosolówski, Albína, and Ludwíka, taking the box in which the coffins were to be placed, drove off in a hired cart. At the cemetery where the children were buried, Albína, falling on her knees by their grave, prayed awhile, but soon rose, dried her eyes, and saying to Rosolówski, " Do what is necessary . . . I can't !" stepped aside.

Rosolówski and Ludwíka moved the gravestone and dug up the top of the grave with spades, so that it looked as if it had been opened. When this was done they called Albína ; and returned home with the box full of earth.

The day fixed for their departure arrived. Rosolówski rejoiced at the success of the enterprise now so nearly accomplished. Ludwíka had baked pastry and cakes for the journey, and, repeating her usual asseveration, " By my mother !" declared her heart was bursting with fear and joy. Migoúrski was glad of his deliverance from the garret where he had spent more than a month, but yet gladder at Albína's animation and joy of life. She seemed to have forgotten all former griefs and all danger, and came running to him in the garret, beaming with rapturous delight as in the days of her girlhood.

At three in the morning came a Cossack escort, and brought a driver with three horses. Albína and Ludwíka, with their little dog, got into the *tarantás* and sat down on cushions covered with a rug. The Cossack and the driver got on to the box ; Migoúrski, dressed as a peasant, lay at the bottom of the vehicle.

They drove out of the town, and the three good horses drew the *tarantás* along the smooth road, hard as a stone, that ran through an endless uncultivated steppe covered with last year's dry, silvery feather-grass.

X

Albína's heart swelled with hope and elation. Wishing to impart her feelings to someone, she occasionally, smiling slightly, drew Ludwíka's attention by a movement of her head—first to the Cossack's broad back, and then to the bottom of the *tarantás*. Ludwíka sat looking before her fixedly, with a significant expression, and only slightly twitched her lips.

The day was bright. All around spread the boundless desert steppe, its silvery feather-grass glittering in the slanting rays of the morning sun. First on one and then on the other side of the hard road—on which the brisk unshod hoofs of

the Bashkír horses resounded as on asphalt—
appeared little mounds of earth thrown up by
Siberian marmots, with one of the little creatures
sitting up erect and keeping watch. At the approach of danger it would raise the alarm by a
shrill whistle, and disappear down its burrow.
They met but few travellers : only a Cossack
train of carts laden with wheat, or a mounted
Bashkír with whom their Cossack briskly bandied
Tartar words. At each post-station they got
fresh and well-fed horses, and the half-roubles
Albína gave to the drivers made them gallop
full speed all the way—" State-messenger style,"
as they expressed it.

At the first station, when the first driver had
gone away with the horses and his successor had
not yet come with the fresh ones, and the Cossack
had gone into the yard, Albína bent down and
asked her husband how he felt, and whether he
needed anything.

" Splendid ! . . . Quite comfortable ! I want
nothing ; I can easily lie here for two days, if
necessary."

Towards evening they reached the large village
of Dergátchi. That her husband might stretch
his limbs and refresh himself, Albína did not put
up at the post-station, but stopped in an inn-

yard; and, giving some money to the Cossack, sent him at once to buy her some milk and eggs. The *tarantás* stood in a shed, and it was dark in the yard. Setting Ludwíka to watch the Cossack, Albína let her husband out and fed him; and before the Cossack returned he was again in his hiding-place. Albína's spirits rose higher and higher, and she could not restrain her gaiety and delight. Having no one to talk to but Ludwíka, the Cossack, and her dog, Trezórka, she amused herself with them. Ludwíka, in spite of her plainness, suspected all the men she ever met of having amorous designs upon herself; and on this occasion she had the same suspicions of their escort, the sturdy, good-natured Urál Cossack, with unusually bright and kind blue eyes, whose simplicity and good-natured adroitness made him very agreeable to both the women.

Besides Trezórka (at whom Albína shook her finger, not allowing him to sniff under the seat), she now amused herself with Ludwíka's comical coquetting with the Cossack; who, never suspecting the designs attributed to him, smiled at all that was said. Albína, excited by the danger, the success that was attending the accomplishment of her plan, and the air of the steppes, experienced a long-forgotten feeling of childlike joy and

happiness. Migoúrski heard her talking merrily,
and forgetting himself—in spite of the physical
discomfort of his position, which he concealed
from her (he was especially tormented by thirst
and heat)—he rejoiced at her joy.

Towards the evening of the second day, something began to appear in the distance, through
the mist. It was Sarátof and the Vólga. The
Cossack, whose eyes were used to the steppes,
could see the Vólga and a mast, and pointed them
out to Ludwíka—who said she could see them
too ; but Albína could see nothing, and only repeated loudly, that her husband should hear,
" Sarátof . . . Vólga . . ." as if she were talking to
Trezórka ; and so she informed her husband of
all she saw.

XI

Not entering the town, Albína stopped on the
left bank of the Vólga, in the Pokróvsky suburb,
just opposite Sarátof itself. Here she hoped to
be able to speak to her husband during the night,
and even to let him out of his box. But the
Cossack never left the *tarantás* during the whole
of the short spring night, but sat near it in a cart
that stood under the same shed. Ludwíka, by
Albína's orders, remained in the *tarantás*, and

feeling sure it was because of her that the Cossack remained near it, she winked, laughed, and hid her pock-marked face in her kerchief. But Albína saw nothing amusing in this now, and became more and more anxious; wondering why the Cossack remained so persistently near the *tarantás*.

Several times during that short night, in which the evening twilight melted into the twilight of dawn, Albína left the inn, and, passing through a passage which smelt foully, came out into the back porch. The Cossack did not sleep, but sat in the empty cart beside the *tarantás*, with his legs hanging down. Only just before daybreak, when the cocks were already awake and crowing to one another from yard to yard, Albína went down and found time to speak to her husband. The Cossack, lying stretched out in the cart, was snoring. She came carefully up to the *tarantás*, and knocked at the box.

" Josy !"

No answer.

" Josy ! Josy !" she said louder, quite frightened.

" What's the matter ?" asked Migoúrski, in a sleepy voice, inside the box.

" Why didn't you answer ?"

" I was asleep," he said, and by the sound of his voice she knew that he was smiling.

" Well, can I get out ?" he asked.

" No ! the Cossack is here ;" and, saying this, she glanced at the Cossack sleeping in the cart.

And, strange to say, though the Cossack was snoring, his kind blue eyes were open. He looked at her, and only when their glances met did he shut his eyes again.

" Was it only my fancy, or was he really awake ?" Albína asked herself. " It must have been my fancy," she thought, and again turned to the box.

" Bear it a bit longer," she said. " Do you want something to eat ?"

" No ; I want to smoke."

Albína looked at the Cossack. He was asleep.

" Yes, I only fancied it," she thought.

" Now I shall go and see the Governor."

" Well, then, good luck to you !"

Albína took a dress from her portmanteau and went into the inn to change the one she was wearing.

Dressed in her best widow's mourning, Albína crossed the Vólga. Hiring an *isvóztchik** on the quay, she drove to the Governor's. The Governor received her. The pretty, smiling Polish widow, speaking excellent French, pleased the

* The Russian equivalent to a cabman.

would-be-young old Governor very much.   He
granted all she asked, and bade her call again next
day, to receive an order to the Mayor of Tsarítsin.

Pleased at the success of her application, and
by the effect she noticed that her attractiveness
produced on the Governor's manners, Albína
returned happy and hopeful.   She descended the
hill in a *tarantás*, driving along the unpaved street
back to the landing.   The sun had risen above
the forest, and its slanting rays played on the
rippling waters of the wide overflow of the river.
Apple-trees, covered with sweet blossoms, appeared like white clouds to right and left.   A
forest of masts was seen along the banks, and
white sails gleamed on the surface of the broad
overflow, ruffled by a gentle breeze.   At the
landing, after some talk with her driver, Albína
inquired whether she could hire a boat to take
her to Astrakhán ; and dozens of noisy, merry
boatmen offered her their services and boats.
She came to an agreement with a man she liked
better than the rest, and went to look at his
boat, that lay among a crowd of others near the
landing.   The boat had a small movable mast
with a sail, and also oars for calm weather.   Two
healthy-looking *bourlák* rowers sat in the boat,
sunning themselves.   The merry, kindly boat-

man advised her not to leave her *tarantás* behind,
but to take off the wheels and place it in the
boat. " There will be just enough room, and it
will be more comfortable for you to sit in it. If
God gives us good weather, we'll run down to
Astrakhán in five days or so."

Having come to terms with the boatman, Albína
bade him come to Lóginof's inn, in the Pokróvsky
suburb, to see the *tarantás* and to receive hand-
money. Everything was succeeding beyond her
expectations. In a rapturously happy mood she
crossed the Vólga, paid her driver, and went
towards the inn-yard.

XII

The Cossack, Daniel Lifánof, belonged to the
Strelétsky Settlement, on the watershed of the
Vólga and the Urál. He was thirty-four, and
was completing the last month of the term of his
army service. At home he had a grandfather, a
man of ninety (who could remember Pougat-
chéf*) ; two brothers ; a sister-in-law (the wife
of an elder brother who had been sent to the
mines for being an Old Believer) ; a wife ; and

* The Cossack leader of a formidable peasant rising.
He was executed in 1775.

two sons. His father had been killed in the war with the French. He was the head of the family. In his homestead they had sixteen horses and two yoke of oxen, and they had a good deal of land sown with wheat. Daniel had served in Órenburg and Kazán. He kept strictly to the Old Faith, did not smoke, would neither eat nor drink out of a vessel used by the Orthodox, and considered his oath sacred. In all his actions he was deliberately, firmly exact ; and giving his whole attention to whatever his superiors set him to do, he never forgot it for a moment until he had done his duty as he understood it. Now he was ordered to escort two Polish women and two coffins to Sarátof, so that no evil should befall them on the way, and they were to travel quietly and not be up to any mischief ; and at Sarátof he was to hand them over honourably to the Authorities.

And so he had brought them safely to Sarátof— little dog, coffins and all. The women, though Poles, were harmless agreeable women, and they did nothing wrong. But here in the Pokróvsky suburb, towards evening, passing by the *tarantás,* he noticed that the little dog jumped inside and whined and wagged its tail, and he thought he heard someone's voice coming from under the

seat of the *tarantás*. One of the Polish women—
the old one—grew frightened on seeing the dog
in the *tarantás*, and caught it and carried it away.

" There's something wrong there," thought the
Cossack, and remained on the lookout. When the
young Polish woman came out in the night to the
tarantás, he pretended to be asleep, and distinctly
heard a man's voice coming from the box. Early
in the morning he went to the police to let them
know that the Polish women entrusted to his care
were not travelling honestly, but were carrying,
instead of coffins, a live man in their box.

When Albína—in her rapturously happy mood,
sure that all was now finished, and that in a few
days they would be free—came to the inn-yard, she
was surprised to see an elegant pair of horses and
two Cossacks at the gates. A crowd had collected
round the gates, and were gazing into the yard.

So full of hope and energy was she, that it did
not occur to her that the pair of horses and the
crowd of people had any connection with her.
She entered the yard, and glancing at once
towards the shed where her *tarantás* stood, she
saw that it was just there that the people were
crowding, and at the same moment she heard
Trezórka barking desperately.

The most terrible thing that could possibly

have happened had actually come to pass! In front of the *tarantás*, in his clean uniform, with buttons, shoulder-straps and patent-leather boots glittering in the sunshine, stood an imposing-looking man, with black whiskers, speaking in a loud, hoarse, commanding voice. In front of him, between two soldiers, dressed as a peasant, and with bits of hay in his tangled hair, stood her Josy, raising and lowering his powerful shoulders as if perplexed by what was going on around him. Trezórka, his hair bristling, quite unconscious that he was the cause of all this misfortune, was barking angrily at the Police Master. When he saw Albína, Migoúrski gave a start and wished to approach her, but the soldiers prevented him.

"Never mind, Albína, never mind!" uttered Migoúrski, with his usual gentle smile.

"Ah! Here's the little lady herself!" said the Police Master. "Come here, please. . . . The coffins of your infants, eh?" he added, winking towards Migoúrski. Albína did not answer, but clutching at her breast, stared open-mouthed and horror-stricken at her husband.

As happens at the moment of death, and in general at the decisive moments of life, a crowd of feelings and thoughts passed through her mind in a single instant, before she had yet realized

or quite believed in her misfortune. The first
feeling was one already long familiar to her—a
feeling of offended pride at seeing her hero-
husband humiliated by these coarse, savage people
who now had him in their power. " How dare
they hold him—the best of all men—in their
power ?" At the same time another feeling—
the consciousness of misfortune—seized her.
This consciousness of her misfortune awoke the
memory of the greatest misfortune of her life—
her children's death. And at once the question
arose : " Why—why were the children taken ?"
And this question suggested another : " Why is
he now perishing and being tormented—he, my
beloved, my husband, the best of men ?" And
then she remembered the shameful punishment
awaiting him, and that it was all her doing.

" What is he to you ? Is he your husband ?"
the Police Master repeated.

" Why ? What for ?" she cried ; and bursting
into hysterical laughter, she fell on the box, which
had been removed from the *tarantás* and now
stood on the ground beside it. Shaking with sobs,
her face bathed in tears, Ludwíka approached her.

" Mistress . . . dear, darling mistress ! . . . By
God, nothing will come of it—nothing ! . . ." she
said, mechanically passing her hand over Albína.

Migoúrski was handcuffed and led out of the yard. Seeing this, Albína ran after him.

" Forgive me ! Forgive me !" she said. " It is my fault—my fault alone !"

" They'll soon find out whose fault it is ! Your turn will come, too," said the Police Master, and he pushed her aside with his arm.

Migoúrski was taken to the ferry, and Albína followed him without knowing why, paying no heed to Ludwíka's dissuasions.

The Cossack, Daniel Lifánof, stood all this while by the wheels of the *tarantás,* looking gloomily now at the Police Master, now at Albína, now at his own feet. After Migoúrski had been led away, Trezórka, who had got used to Lifánof on the journey, began wagging his tail and caressing him. The Cossack suddenly moved away from the *tarantás,* pulled off his cap, threw it violently on the ground, shoved Trezórka aside with his boot, and went into the inn. There he demanded vódka, and drank day and night till he had drunk all the money he had, and all his clothes as well. Only when he came to himself in a ditch, during the second night, did he stop thinking about the tormenting problem : Whether he had done well to report to the Authorities about the Polish woman's husband inside the box ?

Migoúrski was tried for attempting to escape, and was condemned to run the gauntlet through a line of 1,000 men. By the intercession of his relations and of Wánda (who had influential connections in Petersburg), his sentence was commuted to one of exile for life to Siberia. Albína followed him. As to Nicholas I, he rejoiced at having crushed the hydra of revolution—not only in Poland, but throughout Europe—and prided himself on having benefited the Russian people by keeping Poland under Russian rule. And men in gold-embroidered uniforms, wearing stars, so applauded him for this, that he sincerely believed himself to be a great man, and his life a great blessing to humanity—especially to the Russian people, to whose perversion and stupefaction he unconsciously directed all his powers.

1906.

VI

GOD'S WAY AND MAN'S

I

I⊤ happened in Russia in the 'seventies, when the struggle between the Revolutionists and the Government was at its height.

The General-Governor of a district in South Russia, a healthy-looking German with drooping moustaches and a cold look on his expressionless face, dressed in a military uniform, with a white cross at his neck, sat one evening in his cabinet, at a table on which were placed four candles with green shades, looking through and signing papers left for him by his secretary.

Among those papers was the death-warrant of Anatole Svetlogoúb, a graduate of the Novorossíysk University, sentenced for taking part in a conspiracy to overthrow the then existing Government. The General, frowning deeply, signed that paper, too. With his white, well-kept fingers, wrinkled by old age and the use of much

soap, he carefully adjusted the edges of the
sheets and laid them aside. The next paper dealt
with the sums assigned for the carriage of prov-
ender. He read this attentively, considering
whether the amounts were correctly or wrongly
calculated, when suddenly he remembered a talk
he had had with his assistant about Svetlogoúb's
case. The General thought that the dynamite
found in Svetlogoúb's possession was not sufficient
proof of criminal intentions ; while the assistant
insisted that besides the dynamite there was
sufficient evidence to prove that Svetlogoúb was
the leader of the gang. And, remembering this,
the General became thoughtful; and his heart,
under the padded coat with facings as stiff as
cardboard, began to beat nervously ; and he
breathed so hard that the large white cross—the
object of his joy and pride—visibly rose and sank
on his breast. The secretary might still be
called back, and the sentence might at least be
delayed, if not remitted.

" Shall I call him back, or shall I not ? "
His heart beat more irregularly. He rang ; and
the courier entered with quick, nervous footsteps.
" Has Iván Matvéitch gone ? "
" No, your Excellency ; he is in the office."
The General's heart now stopped, now beat

quickly. He remembered the warnings of the doctor who had examined him a few days before.

" Above all," the doctor had said, " if you begin to feel that you have a heart, stop working— divert your mind. There is nothing so bad as agitation. On no account allow yourself to be agitated."

" Shall I call him, your Excellency ?"

" No, it is not necessary," answered the General. " Yes," said he to himself, " nothing is so agitating as indecision. It is signed and done with. . . . ' *Ein jeder macht sich sein Bett und muss d'rauf schlafen* ' "*: he repeated his favourite proverb. " Besides, it is not my business. I only fulfil the Supreme Will,† and must stand above that kind of consideration," he added, frowning to awaken in himself the cruelty which was not natural to him.

And here he remembered his last interview with the Tsar—how the latter had fixed his cold, icy look on him and had said : " I trust you ! As in war you did not spare yourself, so you must act with the same firmness now in the fight with the ' red ones,' and must not allow yourself to be either deceived or frightened. . . . Good-bye !" Then

---

* " Each man makes his bed, and must sleep on it."
† The Tsar's orders are so called, in official parlance.

the Tsar had embraced him, offering his shoulder
to the General to kiss. The General recalled the
words with which he had answered the Tsar :
" My one desire is to give my life to serve my
Emperor and my country !"

And as he recalled the feeling of servile emotion
which the consciousness of his self-sacrificing
loyalty to his Sovereign had evoked in him, he
drove from his mind the thought which for a
moment had disturbed him—signed the rest of
the papers, and rang again.

" Is tea ready ?" he asked.

" It is just being served, your Excellency."

" All right . . . you may go."

The Governor sighed deeply, and rubbed the
place where his heart was. Then, heavily tread-
ing through the large empty hall, with its freshly
polished parquet-floor, he went towards the
drawing-room, whence came the sound of voices.

The General's wife had visitors : the Governor
and his wife ; an old Princess, an ardent patriot ;
and an officer of the Guards—the fiancé of his
last unmarried daughter. His wife, a thin-
lipped, cold-faced woman, sat at a low table, on
which tea was laid, a silver teapot standing on
the top of the samovár. She was speaking with
affected sadness of her anxiety about her hus-

band's health, to the Governor's wife—a lady who gave herself the airs of a young woman.

"Every day fresh information brings to light conspiracies and all sorts of dreadful things. . . . And it all falls on Basil—he has to decide everything."

"Oh, don't mention it!" said the Princess. "*Je deviens féroce quand je pense à cette maudite engeance !*"*

"Yes, yes . . . it's awful! Will you believe it ? He works twelve hours a day, and with his weak heart, too. I really am afraid. . . ."

Seeing her husband enter, she did not finish the sentence.

"Oh yes, you must hear him! Barbini is a wonderful tenor," she said, smiling amiably at the Governor's wife. She referred to a singer newly arrived in Russia, and did so as naturally as though he had been the sole subject of their conversation.

The General's daughter, a plump, pretty young girl, was sitting with her fiancé behind a Chinese screen at the other end of the drawing-room. They both rose and went up to her father.

"Dear me! Why, we have not yet seen one

* "I become savage when I think of that accursed brood !"

another to-day !" said the General, kissing his
daughter and pressing her fiancé's hand.

After greeting his guests, the General sat down
at a small table, and began talking with the
Governor about the latest news.

" No, no ! You must not talk business—it is
forbidden !" the General's wife said, interrupting
the Governor. " Ah . . . and, as luck will have
it, here is Kópyef : he will tell us something
amusing !"

And Kópyef, noted for his gaiety and wit, did
tell them the latest anecdote, which made everybody laugh.

II

" No, no ! It cannot be, it cannot ! . . . Let
me go !" Svetlogoúb's mother shouted pierc-
ingly, struggling to free herself from the grasp
of the schoolmaster—her son's friend—and of the
doctor, who were trying to keep her back.

Svetlogoúb's mother was a nice-looking middle-
aged woman, with grey curls and a star of wrinkles
near each eye.

The schoolmaster, when he heard that the
death-warrant was signed, wanted to prepare her
gently for the terrible news ; but he had hardly
begun to speak about her son when, by the tone

of his voice and his timid look, she guessed that what she dreaded had really happened. This took place in a small room in the best hotel in the town.

"Oh dear ! Why do you hold me ? Let go !" she shouted, freeing herself from the doctor —an old friend of the family, who with one hand held her by her thin elbow, and with the other put a bottle of medicine on the table which stood before the sofa. She was glad they held her, because she felt that she ought to do something, but did not know what to do, and was afraid of herself.

"Don't be so agitated. . . . Here, take these valerian drops," said the doctor, handing her a glass of turbid liquid.

She suddenly grew quiet, and, bent almost double, her head drooping on to her hollow chest, she closed her eyes and sank on to the sofa.

She remembered how, three months ago, her son had taken leave of her with a look of mystery and sorrow on his face. Then she recalled him as an eight-year-old boy, dressed in a velvet jacket, with bare legs and long fair ringlets.

"And him . . . him, that very boy . . . they are going to destroy ! . . ."

She jumped up, pushing away the table, and

tore herself from the doctor ; but on reaching the
door she again sank on to a chair.

"And they say there is a God! . . . What
God is He, if He allows it ? . . . May the devil
take Him, that God!" she screamed, now sobbing,
now breaking into hysterical laughter. "To
hang him . . . who gave up all—his whole career,
all his property—to others . . . gave it all to the
people! . . ." She, who had formerly reproached
her son for this, was now speaking of his self-
abnegation as a merit. "And him—him . . .
they will do it to him! . . . And you say there is
a God!" she cried.

"But I do not say anything : I only ask you
to take these drops."

"I want nothing. . . . Ha, ha, ha!" she laughed
and sobbed, beside herself with despair.

Towards night she was so exhausted with
suffering that she could neither speak nor weep,
but only stared in front of her with a fixed, insane
gaze. The doctor injected morphia, and she fell
asleep.

It was a dreamless sleep, but the awakening
was worse than what had gone before. What
appeared most terrible was that people could be
so cruel: not only those dreadful Generals with
their shaved cheeks, and the gendarmes, but

everybody, everybody : the maid who came to do the room, with her quiet face, and the people in the next room, who greeted one another cheerfully, and laughed as if nothing had happened.

III

Svetlogoúb had lived through a great deal during the three months of his solitary confinement. From his very childhood he had unconsciously felt the injustice of the exceptional position he held as a rich man ; and though he tried to stifle this feeling, often when he came in contact with the poverty of the common people—or sometimes even when he was particularly happy and comfortable himself—he felt rather ashamed of his relation to the people : to peasants, old men, women, and children, who were born, grew up and died, not only without knowing the pleasures he enjoyed, but without even understanding them, and never free from toil and hardship. When he had finished his studies at the University—in order to liberate himself from the consciousness of this injustice— he organized a school in the village on his estate : a model school, a Co-operative Store, and a Home for the aged poor. Yet, strange to say, when occupied with all this, he felt even more ashamed than when he was at supper with his comrades or when he purchased an expensive riding horse. He felt that it was not the right thing, and, even worse than that : there seemed to be something bad about it, something morally impure.

In one of these fits of disillusionment about his village activities he went to Kief, where he met a fellow-University student. Three years later that fellow-student was shot in the moat of Kief fortress.

That comrade, an ardent and extremely gifted young man, drew Svetlogoúb into a society the object of which was to enlighten the people, to awaken them to a consciousness of their rights, and to form them into federated groups aiming at freeing the people from the landlords and the Government. His conversation with this man and this man's friends, seemed to ripen into a clear perception all that Svetlogoúb had been vaguely feeling. He understood now what he had to do. Without breaking off his intercourse with his new comrades, he returned to the country, and there began quite a fresh line of activity. He himself took the place of schoolmaster, arranged adult classes, read books and pamphlets to the peasants, and explained to them their true position.

Besides all this, he published illegal* books and pamphlets for the people, and gave all that, without taking anything from his mother, he could give for the formation of similar centres in other villages.

From the first, Svetlogoúb was faced in this activity by two unexpected obstacles : the first was the fact that the majority of the people treated his preaching with indifference, or even with a certain contempt.   Only exceptional men (often men of doubtful morality) listened and sympathized with him.   The other obstacle came from the side of the Government.   They closed his school; and the police searched his house and the dwellings of all who were connected with him, and confiscated books and papers.

Svetlogoúb was too indignant with the second obstacle—the senseless and humiliating oppression of the Government—to pay much attention to the first.   The same was felt by his comrades who were active in other centres, and the feeling of irritation they fomented in one another reached such a pitch of intensity that the great majority of their Group decided to fight the Government by force.   The head of that Group

---

* That is to say, books and pamphlets which, for political reasons, the censor would not sanction, and which it was therefore dangerous to publish.

was a certain Mezhenétsky, regarded by everybody as a man of indomitable power, incontestable logic, and entirely devoted to the cause of Revolution.

Svetlogoúb submitted to this man's influence, and with the same energy with which he had worked among the people, now gave himself up to terrorist activity. That activity was dangerous, but the danger more than anything else attracted Svetlogoúb.

He said to himself : " Victory or martyrdom . . . and if it is to be martyrdom it will still be victory in the future !" And the fire that had been kindled within him, remained not only un-extinguished during the seven years of his revolutionary activity, but fanned by the affection and esteem of those among whom he moved, burned more and more fiercely.

He attached no importance to the fact that he had given away for the cause almost all his fortune (inherited from his father), nor to the hardships and privations which he often had to encounter in the course of his activity. The only thing that grieved him was the sorrow he was causing to his mother and her ward—a girl who lived with her and loved him.

At last one of his comrades—a terrorist whom he did not much like, a disagreeable man—when

tracked by the police, asked Svetlogoúb to hide
some dynamite in his house. Just because he
did not like that comrade, Svetlogoúb agreed ;
and the next day the police searched the house
and found the dynamite. When asked how the
dynamite had come into his possession, Svetlogoúb
refused to answer.

And now the martyrdom he expected began.
At that time, after so many of his friends had
been executed, imprisoned, or exiled, and so
many women had suffered, Svetlogoúb almost
desired martyrdom. During the first moments
after his arrest and examination he felt a peculiar
exultation and almost joy.

He felt this while he was being undressed and
searched, and while he was being led to prison,
and when the iron doors were locked upon him.
But when one day passed, and another, and a
third, a week, two weeks, three weeks, in the
dirty, damp, vermin-infested cell, in loneliness
and enforced idleness, varied only by cheerless
or bad news, which his comrades and fellow-
prisoners communicated by tapping on the walls
of their cells ; and by occasional examinations by
cold, hostile men who tried to torment him into
incriminating his comrades, his moral—and with
it his physical—strength gradually began to give

way. He became despondent and, as he said to
himself, longed for this insufferable position to
end one way or another. His despondency was
aggravated by doubts of his own endurance. In
the second month of his incarceration he de-
tected himself thinking of revealing the whole
truth : anything to be free ! He was appalled at
this weakness, but could no longer find in himself
his former strength ; and, hating and despising
himself, became more despondent than ever.
But what was most terrible was the fact that, in
prison, he began to regret the youthful powers and
pleasures he had sacrificed so lightly when he was
free, and which now appeared so enchanting that
he almost repented of doing what he had once
considered right, and sometimes even of the
whole of his activity. Thoughts came to him
of how happy he would be if he had liberty,
living in the country or abroad, free, among
loving and beloved friends ; how he might marry
her, or perhaps another, and with her might live
a simple, joyous, bright life.

IV

On one of the painfully monotonous days of
the second month of Svetlogoúb's imprisonment,

the inspector, while making his daily round, handed him a little book with a gilt cross on its brown binding, saying that the Governor's wife had visited the prison and had left some Testaments, and that permission had been granted to distribute them among the prisoners. Svetlogoúb thanked him, and smiled slightly as he put the book on the little table screwed fast to the wall. When the inspector had gone, Svetlogoúb informed his neighbour by tapping that the inspector had been, and had said nothing new, but had left a Testament. The neighbour replied that he also had received one.

After dinner Svetlogoúb opened the book, the pages of which stuck together from the damp, and began to read. He had never before read the gospels as a book, and knew them only as he had gone through them with the Scripture teacher at school, and as the priests and deacons chanted them in church.

" Chapter i. : The book of the generation of Jesus Christ the son of David, the son of Abraham . . . Isaac begat Jacob, Jacob begat Judah . .. " and he went on to read : " Zorubbabel begat Abiud. . . ."

All this was just what he expected—some kind of involved, worthless jargon. Had he not been in prison he could not have read a single page to the end ; but here he went on reading for the sake of the mechanical act of reading—" Just like Gógol's Petroúsha," he thought to himself. He read the first chapter, about the Virgin Birth and the prophecy which said that the new-born child would be named Emmanuel, which meant " God with us."

" But where does the prophecy come in ?" he thought, and went on reading the second chapter, about the wandering star ; and the third, about John who ate locusts ; and the fourth, about some devil who suggested to Christ a gymnastic performance from a roof. All this seemed so uninteresting to him that, in spite of the dulness of the prison, he was about to close the book and start on his usual evening occupation—flea-hunting on the shirt he took off—when suddenly he remembered how at an examination of the fifth class at school he had forgotten one of the Beatitudes, and how the rosy-faced, curly-headed priest had suddenly grown angry and given him a bad mark. He could not recollect the text, so he began reading the Beatitudes. " Blessed are the poor in spirit : for theirs is the kingdom of heaven," he read. " This might relate also to us," he thought. " Blessed are they that have been

16

persecuted for righteousness' sake : for theirs is
the kingdom of heaven.   Blessed are ye when
men shall reproach you, and persecute you. . . .
Rejoice, and be exceeding glad : for great is your
reward in heaven : for so persecuted they the
prophets which were before you.   Ye are the
salt of the earth : but if the salt have lost its
savour, wherewith shall it be salted ?   It is
thenceforth good for nothing, but to be cast out
and trodden under foot of men."

" This quite plainly refers to us," he thought,
and read farther.   When he had read the whole
of the fifth chapter, he became thoughtful.   " Do
not be angry, don't commit adultery, bear with
evil, love your enemies. . . .   Yes, if all men
lived so," he thought, " there would be no need
of revolutions."   As he read farther he entered
more and more into the spirit of the passages
which were quite comprehensible ; and the longer
he read the more the idea grew on him that
something very important was said in that book—
something important, simple and touching ; something he had never heard before, and which yet
seemed to have long been familiar.

" Then said Jesus unto his disciples, If any
man would come after me, let him deny himself,
and take up his cross, and follow me.   For who-

soever would save his life shall lose it : and whosoever shall lose his life for my sake shall find it. For what shall a man be profited, if he shall gain the whole world, and lose his own soul ?" (Matt. xvi. 24, 25, 26).

" Yes, yes—that is it !" he suddenly exclaimed, with tears in his eyes. " That is just what I wished to do. . . . Yes, I wished just that : just to give my soul, not to keep it safe, but to give it. . . . That is where joy lies—that is life ! . . . I have done a great deal for other people's sake, for the sake of human approbation—not the approbation of the crowd, but for the good opinion of those I respected and loved : Natásha and Dmítry Shelómof. And then I doubted and was agitated. I felt at ease only when I did something my soul demanded—when I wished to give myself, my whole self."

From that moment Svetlogoúb spent most of his time reading and pondering what he read in that book. This reading not only evoked in him a glow of tender emotion which carried him beyond the conditions in which he found himself, but also evoked an activity of mind such as he had never before experienced. He wondered why people did not all live as they were told to in that book. " After all, to live so, is good not

for one only, but for all. We only need live
like that, and there will be no sorrow and no
want, only blessedness."

" If only this would end—if only I could be
free once more," he sometimes thought. " After
all, they will let me out sooner or later, or send
me to penal servitude — no matter which. It
is possible to live like that anywhere . . . and
I will live so ! I can and must live so . . .
not to live so is madness !"

V

One day when he was in that joyous, exalted
state, the inspector came into his cell at an unusual hour, and asked him if he was comfortable,
or if he wanted anything. Svetlogoúb was surprised, and unable to understand what this change
of manner meant. He asked for a packet of
cigarettes and some matches, expecting a refusal.
But the inspector replied that he would send
some at once, and a watchman really brought him
a packet of cigarettes and some matches. " Someone has probably interceded for me," thought
Svetlogoúb ; and, having lit a cigarette, began
to pace up and down the cell, considering what
this change might portend.

Next day he was taken up to the court, where he had been several times before. This time, however, he was not examined, but one of the judges, without looking at him, rose from his chair with a paper in his hand. The others also rose. The judge began to read in an unnaturally expressionless voice. Svetlogoúb listened and looked at the judges' faces. They all avoided looking at him, and listened with a significant and depressed expression on their faces. The document said that Anatole Svetlogoúb, for his participation in Revolutionary activity which had for its aim the overthrow, in the near or more distant future, of the existing Government, was sentenced to be deprived of all his rights, and to death by hanging.

Svetlogoúb listened and understood the words spoken by the official. He noticed the absurdity of the wording, " in the near or more distant future," and the depriving of a man sentenced to death of all his rights ; but he did not in the least understand the significance to himself of what had been read.

Only much later, when he was told that he might go, and was out in the street with a gendarme, did the meaning of the declaration he had just heard begin to dawn upon him.

" That's not it . . . that's not it. . . . It can't be true ! It's absurd !" he said to himself, as he sat in the carriage that was taking him back to prison. He felt so full of vitality that he could not imagine death, could not connect the consciousness of his " I " with death—with the absence of that " I."

When he returned to his cell he sat down on his bed, and closing his eyes, tried to imagine what awaited him, and could not manage to do so. He could not at all imagine that he would not be, nor that people could wish to kill him. " Me, young, kind, happy, loved by so many," he thought, remembering his mother's and Natásha's affection for him, as well as that of his friends. " And they will kill me, hang me ! . . . Who will do it ? Why ? . . . And then what will there be when I am not ? . . . It's impossible . . ." he said to himself.

The inspector came in. Svetlogoúb did not hear him enter.

" Who is it ? What do you want ?" asked Svetlogoúb, not recognizing him. " Ah, it's you ! . . . When is it to be ?" he asked.

" I do not know," answered the inspector, and, having stood still for a moment, suddenly began, in an insinuating, gentle voice :

" The priest is here . . . he would like to . . . to prep . . . he would like to see you."

" I don't want to—it is unnecessary ! I want nothing. . . . Go away !" exclaimed Svetlogoúb.

" Don't you want to write to anybody ? . . . You can," said the inspector.

" Yes, yes ! Send what is necessary. I will write."

The inspector went away.

" That means to-morrow morning," thought Svetlogoúb. " They always behave like that. To-morrow morning I shall not be . . . no, it is impossible ! It's a dream !"

But the watchman came in—the real, familiar watchman—and brought two pens, an inkstand, a packet of notepaper, and some blue envelopes, and moved the stool to the table. All this was reality, and not a dream.

" I must not think . . . only not think. Yes, I will write to Mother," thought Svetlogoúb, and sat down on the stool and at once began.

" My own dear !" he wrote, and burst into tears. " Forgive me—forgive me all the grief I have caused you. Whether I was deluded or not, I could not act otherwise. I only ask you to forgive me !"—" But I have already written this. . . . Well, anyhow, there is no time to alter it now."—" Do not sorrow on my account," he continued. " A little sooner or a little later, is it not all the same ? I am not frightened, nor do I repent of what I have done. I could not act otherwise. Only do you forgive me ! And do not be angry with them—neither with those with whom I worked nor with those who are executing me. Neither the former nor the latter could act otherwise. Forgive them, for they know not what they do ! I dare not say these words about myself, but they are in my soul, and lift me up and calm me. Forgive me ! I kiss your dear, wrinkled, old hands !"

Two tears fell one after another and spread on the paper.

" I am crying, not with grief or fear, but with deep emotion before the most solemn moment of my life, and because I love you. Do not reproach my friends, but love them—especially Próhorof, because he was the cause of my death. It is so joyful to love one who is not exactly guilty, but whom one might reproach and hate ! To learn to love a man of that kind—an enemy— is such happiness ! Tell Natásha that her love was my comfort and joy. I did not fully realize it, but was conscious of it in the depths of my soul. It was easier for me to live, knowing that she existed and loved me. Now I have said everything. Good-bye!"

He folded the letter, sealed it, and sat down on his bed, folding his hands on his knees and swallowing his tears.

He could still not believe he was about to die. He asked himself several times whether he was not asleep, and vainly tried to wake up. And this thought gave rise to another : Whether life in this world is not all a dream, out of which the awaking is death ? And if this be so, whether consciousness in this life is not merely an awakening out of the sleep of a former, unremembered life ? So that this existence does not begin here, but is only a new form of life. " I shall die and enter into a new form." He liked this idea, but when he tried to use it as a support, he felt that neither it, nor any kind of idea whatever, could remove the fear of death. At last he grew tired of thinking ; his brain would no longer work. He shut his eyes and long sat without thinking.

He read his letter over again, and, seeing the name of Próhorof at the end, he remembered that his letter might be read by the officials— would in all probability be read—and would lead to Próhorof's destruction.

" O God, what have I done ?" he suddenly

exclaimed; and, tearing the letter into strips, he began carefully burning them over the lamp.

He was in despair when he sat down to write; but now he felt calm—almost happy. He took another sheet of paper, and again began writing. Thoughts came thronging one after another into his head.

" Dear, darling mother," he wrote, and his eyes were again misty with tears so that he had to wipe them with the sleeve of his prison coat in order to see what he was writing. " How little I knew myself and all the strength of love and gratitude to you which always dwelt in my heart ! Now I know and feel it, and always when I recall our differences, and the unkind words I have said to you, I am pained and ashamed, and can hardly understand it. Forgive me, and remember only the good, if there was any in me ! I am not afraid of death. To speak frankly, I do not understand it or believe in it. After all, if death—annihilation—exists, is it not all the same whether we die thirty years or thirty minutes sooner or later ? And if there is no death, then it is quite indifferent whether it happens sooner or later."

" But why am I philosophizing ?" he thought. " I must say what I said in the other letter— something good at the end. Yes. . . . ' Do not

reproach my friends, but love them—especially
the one who was the involuntary cause of my
death. Kiss Natásha for me, and tell her that I
have always loved her.' "

" What is it ? What is going to happen ?" he
thought again, remembering. " Nothing ? No,
not nothing. . . . What, then ?"

And suddenly it grew quite clear to him that
for a living man there were, and could be, no
answers to these questions.

" Then why am I putting these questions to
myself ? Why ? Yes, why ? I must not question, but live—live, as I was living just now while
writing this letter. Have we not all been sentenced to death long ago, and yet we go on
living ? We live happily . . . joyfully . . . when
we love. Yes, when we love. . . . While I was
writing, I loved and felt happy, and I must go
on living so. That is possible everywhere and
always—when free and when in prison, to-day
and to-morrow, till the end."

He longed to speak to someone gently and
lovingly at once, and knocked at the door. When
the sentinel looked in at his window, he asked him
what the time was, and if he would soon be re-
lieved ; but the sentinel did not answer. Then
he asked for the inspector.

The inspector came, and wanted to know what he desired. " Here—I have written to my mother. Please let her have it ;" and at the thought of his mother the tears again filled his eyes.

The inspector took the letter, promising to forward it, and was going away ; but Svetlogoúb stopped him.

" Wait a minute !" he said, holding him affectionately by his sleeve. " You are kind—why do you stay in such a dismal service ?"

The inspector smiled an unnatural, piteous smile, and hanging his head, he said :

" One has to live."

" Give up this post ! It is always possible to find something. . . . You are so kind—perhaps I might . . ."

The inspector suddenly sobbed, quickly turned away, and went out, banging the door after him.

This agitation increased Svetlogoúb's loving emotion, and forcing back tears of joy, he began pacing up and down the cell—no longer experiencing any fear, but only a feeling of tenderness which lifted him above the world. The question of what would happen to him after death, which he had tried so hard and yet had been unable to solve, now seemed solved for him, and not by any decided, reasoned answer, but by the realization of the real life within himself.

He recalled the words of the Gospels : " Verily, verily, I say unto you, Except a grain of wheat fall into the earth and die, it abideth by itself alone ; but if it die, it beareth much fruit."— " Here am I also falling into the earth—yes, ' verily, verily,' " he repeated.

" I'd better sleep," he suddenly thought, " that my strength may not fail me to-morrow ;" and he lay down, closed his eyes, and immediately fell asleep.

At six o'clock he woke up, still under the influence of a bright, merry dream. He had dreamt that he was with a little fair-haired girl, climbing wide-spreading trees covered with ripe, black cherries, which he picked into a large brass basin. The cherries missed the basin and rolled on the ground, and some sort of strange animals—something like cats—ran after them and threw them up into the air ; while the little girl looked on, shaking with ringing, infectious laughter, so that Svetlogoúb also laughed merrily in his sleep, without knowing why. Suddenly the basin slipped out of the girl's hands, and Svetlogoúb tried to catch it, but missed it. The brass basin, clanging as it knocked against the branches, fell to the ground, and he awoke smiling and listening to the still-continued clanging of the basin. This clanging was the noise made by the drawing of the iron bolts in the corridor. He heard the sound of footsteps, and the clanking of rifles outside, and suddenly he remembered everything. "Oh, to fall asleep again!" thought Svetlogoúb; but that was no longer possible. The steps approached his door. He heard the grating of the key feeling for the keyhole, and the creaking of the door as it opened.

A gendarme officer, the inspector, and the convoy soldiers came in.

"Death? Well, what of it? I will go. . . . It is a good thing—everything is good," thought Svetlogoúb, and he felt the tenderly solemn mood returning, which he had experienced the evening before.

VI

An old man belonging to a "Priestless" sect, who had lost faith in his leaders and was seeking the truth, was confined in the same prison as Svetlogoúb. He denied not only the Church of Níkon,* but also the Government that had existed since the days of Peter the Great, whom

* The Patriarch whose reforms caused a great schism.

he regarded as Antichrist. He called the Tsar's Government, "Snuff-rule,"* and boldly denounced priests and officials. For this he had been tried, kept in gaol, and sent from prison to prison. He was not disturbed by the fact that he had lost his liberty, that the inspectors abused him, that he was manacled, that his fellow-prisoners mocked him, that they—as well as the Authorities—denied God, quarrelled with one another, and defiled His image within themselves in all sorts of ways : he had seen all that when he was free, everywhere in the world outside. He knew that it all resulted from people having lost the true faith and gone astray, like blind puppies away from their mother. And yet he knew that a true faith existed, because he felt it in his heart. He sought it everywhere, but was most hopeful of finding it in the Revelation of St. John the Divine.

"He that is unjust, let him be unjust still : and he which is filthy, let him be filthy still : and he that is righteous, let him be righteous

---

* A term of contempt, and an allusion both to the Government's tobacco revenue and to the fact that smoking was introduced into Russia in Peter the Great's time, to the scandal of the Old Believers, who dwell on the text that : "Not that which entereth into a man, defileth him, but that (smoke) which cometh out of him."

still : and he that is holy, let him be holy still. And, behold, I come quickly ; and my reward is with me, to give every man according as his work shall be " (Rev. xxii. 11, 12).

And he was always reading this mystic book and expecting every moment him who was to come, who would not only reward every man according to his works, but would reveal Divine truth to man.

On the day of Svetlogoúb's execution this man heard the drums beat, and, having climbed to the window, saw a car arrive, and a youth with waving curls and eyes full of light, who smilingly mounted the car.

The youth held a book in his small white hand. He pressed the book to his heart, and the sectarian knew it was a Testament, and as he nodded to the prisoners at the windows he exchanged a look with the old man. The horses started, and the car, with the youth who appeared bright as an angel, and the guard who surrounded him, rattling over the stones, passed out of the gate.

The sectarian got down from the window and sat on his bunk, meditating. " That one knows the truth," he thought. " Antichrist's servants will strangle him with a rope for it, that he should not reveal it to anyone."

VII

It was a dull autumn morning. The sun was invisible, and a warm, moist breeze came from the sea.

The fresh air, the sight of houses, the town, the horses, the people who looked at him, all distracted Svetlogoúb. Sitting on the bench of the car, with his back to the driver, he involuntarily examined the faces of the convoy soldiers and of the people in the streets.

It was early morning. The streets along which he was driven were almost empty, and they only met a few workmen. Some bricklayers with aprons on, all bespattered with mortar, who met the car, stopped and turned back again as it passed, as though to accompany it. One of them said something, then waved his hand, and then they all turned back again and went to their work. Some carters, carting loads of rattling iron bars, moved their heavy horses to let the car pass, and stood looking at Svetlogoúb with perplexed curiosity. One of them took off his cap and crossed himself. A cook with a white apron, a cap on her head and a basket on her arm, came out of a gate ; but, seeing the car, she quickly turned back and ran out again with

another woman, and they breathlessly followed
the car with very wide-open eyes as long as
it was in sight. A tattered, unshaven, grey-
haired man explained something with energetic
and evidently disapproving gestures to a porter,
as he pointed to Svetlogoúb. Two boys ran after
the car at a trot, caught up with it, and with
their faces turned towards it, went along the
pavement without looking where they were going.
The older one walked with big strides, the little
one, bareheaded, clung to the elder, looking at
the car with frightened eyes, stumbling on his
short legs, and keeping up with the other with
difficulty. When Svetlogoúb's eyes met those of
the little boy, Svetlogoúb nodded to him. This
action of the terrible man in the car staggered the
boy so much that, staring with wide-open eyes
and open mouth, he was just beginning to cry.
Then Svetlogoúb kissed his hand to him with a
kind smile, and the boy suddenly and unex-
pectedly answered with a sweet, kindly smile.

During the whole of the drive the consciousness
of what awaited him did not disturb Svetlogoúb's
calm and solemn state of mind.

Only when the car approached the gallows and
he was helped out, and saw the posts with the
crossbeam, and the cord that hung from it

slightly swinging in the breeze, he experienced
an almost physical blow on his heart. He suddenly felt sick. But this did not last long. Beneath the scaffold he saw black rows of soldiers
with guns ; officers were walking in front of them ;
and as soon as they began helping him down from
the car, he heard an unexpected rattle of beating
drums, which made him start. Behind the rows
of soldiers Svetlogoúb perceived carriages with
ladies and gentlemen, who had come to see the
sight. All this surprised him for a moment, but
he immediately recollected himself as he had been
before his imprisonment, and felt sorry these
people did not know what he now knew. " But
they will know. . . . I shall die, but truth will
not die. They too will know ! And how happy
everybody—not I—but they all might be, and
will be !"

They led him on to the scaffold, an officer
following. The drums became silent, and the
officer, in an unnatural tone, which sounded
peculiarly weak amid the open fields and after
the rattle of the drums, read the same stupid
words of the sentence that had been read to him
in court : about his being deprived of all his
rights—he whom they were about to kill !—and
about the near and more distant future. " Oh,

why, why do they do all this ?" thought Svetlogoúb. " What a pity it is that they don't know,
and that I can no longer tell them of it ! But
they will know—everyone will know. . . ."

A lean priest, with thin long hair, in a lilac
cassock, with a small gilt cross on his breast and a
large silver one in his weak white thick-veined
hand encircled by a black velvet cuff, drew near
to Svetlogoúb.

" Merciful Lord ! . . ." he began, changing the
cross from his left to his right hand, and holding it out to Svetlogoúb. Svetlogoúb shuddered
and moved aside. He was on the point of saying
some angry words to this priest, who was taking
part in the deed that was being done to him and
was at the same time speaking of mercy ; but,
recollecting the words of the Gospels, " they
know not what they do," he made an effort and
mildly uttered the words : " Excuse me, I do
not want it. Please forgive me, but really I
don't want it, thank you !"

He held out his hand to the priest, who changed
the cross back into his left hand, and after pressing
Svetlogoúb's hand, descended from the scaffold,
trying not to look him in the face. The drums
began to roll again, deafening every other sound.
After the priest, a man of medium height with

sloping shoulders and muscular arms, and wearing
a pea-jacket over his Russian shirt, approached
Svetlogoúb with rapid steps, shaking the boards
of the scaffold. This man glanced rapidly at
Svetlogoúb, came quite close up to him, envelop-
ing him in a disagreeable odour of spirits and
perspiration, and with clutching fingers took
him by the arms just above the wrists, and
pressing them together so that they hurt, twisted
them behind Svetlogoúb's back and tied them
there tightly. After that, the hangman stood
for a moment or two as if considering something,
looking first at Svetlogoúb, then at some things
he had brought with him and had put down on
the scaffold, and then at the rope dangling above.
Having made his observations, he went up to the
rope, did something to it, and moved Svetlogoúb
forward, nearer to it and to the edge of the
scaffold.

Just as, at the time when the sentence had been
pronounced on him, Svetlogoúb could not realize
the importance of what was being said, so now he
could not comprehend the full meaning of the
moment that awaited him, and looked on with
wonder at the hangman, who was fulfilling his
terrible task hurriedly, deftly, and in a preoccu-
pied manner. The hangman had a most ordinary

Russian workman's face; not cruel, but engrossed, like that of a man trying to do a necessary and complicated job as accurately as possible.

"Move a bit nearer here . . ." he muttered in a hoarse voice, pushing Svetlogoúb towards the gallows. Svetlogoúb moved closer.

"Lord, help—have mercy on me!" he said.

Svetlogoúb had not believed in God, and had often even laughed at people who did; nor did he believe in Him now, for he was unable not only to express Him in words, but even to comprehend Him with his mind. But what he now meant, and addressed himself to, he knew to be the most real of all that he did know. He also knew that to address himself to It was necessary and important, and he knew this, because It instantly strengthened and calmed him.

He moved towards the gallows, and involuntarily cast a look round at the soldiers and at the motley crowd of onlookers, and again he thought: "Why, why do they do it?" And he pitied them and himself, and tears came to his eyes.

"And are you not sorry for me?" he said, his glance meeting the executioner's bold grey eyes.

The executioner stopped for a moment. His face suddenly turned cruel.

"Get along! Talking!..." he muttered, and quickly stooping down to where his coat and a linen bag lay, with an adroit movement of his arms he embraced Svetlogoúb from behind and threw a linen sack over his head, and drew it hurriedly halfway down his back and chest.

"Into Thy hands I commit my spirit," thought Svetlogoúb, recalling the words of the Gospels.

His spirit did not struggle against death, but his strong young body would not accept it, would not submit, and wanted to rebel.

He wished to shout and to tear himself away, but at that very moment he felt a push, lost his equilibrium, felt animal terror and choking, and a noise in his head, and then everything vanished.

Svetlogoúb's body hung swinging by the cord. His shoulders twice rose and fell.

After waiting a minute or two, the executioner, frowning gloomily, put both hands on the shoulders of the corpse and pushed it downwards with a powerful movement. And the corpse became perfectly still, except for a slow swinging movement of the big doll, with the unnaturally forward-stooping head inside the sack and the outstretched legs in prison stockings.

Descending from the scaffold, the executioner

told his chief that the body might now be taken down and buried.

In an hour's time the body was taken down from the gallows, and removed to the unconsecrated cemetery. The executioner had done what he wished and what he had undertaken to do. But it had not been an easy task to fulfil. Svetlogoúb's words, " And are you not sorry for me ?" would not leave his head. He was a murderer and a convict, and the post of hangman gave him comparative freedom and luxury ; but from that day he refused to fulfil the duties he had undertaken, and drank not only all the money he had received for the execution, but also his comparatively good clothing, and finished by being put into a penitentiary and afterwards into the hospital.

VIII

One of the leaders of the Revolutionary Terrorist party, Ignatius Mezhenétsky, the same who had drawn Svetlogoúb into his terrorist activity, was being transported from the Province where he had been arrested, to Petersburg. The old man who had seen Svetlogoúb taken to execution happened to be in the same prison. He was being transported to Siberia. He still continued to seek for the true faith, and sometimes remembered the bright-faced youth who had smiled so joyfully on his way to death.

When he heard that a comrade of that youth— a man holding the same faith—had been brought to the prison, the sectarian was very glad, and persuaded the watchman to let him see Svetlogoúb's friend.

In spite of the rigorous prison discipline, Mezhenétsky never ceased intercourse with the members of his party, and was every day expecting news about the progress of a plot he himself had originated, to undermine and blow up the Emperor's train. Calling to mind some details he had omitted, he was now trying to find means to communicate them to his adherents. When the watchman came into his cell and guardedly whispered in his ear that one of the convicts wished to see him, he was very pleased, thinking that that interview might furnish him with a chance of communicating with his party.

" Who is he ?" he asked.

" A peasant."

" What does he want ?"

" He wants to have a talk about faith."

Mezhenétsky smiled. " All right ; send him to me," he said. " These sectarians," he thought,

" also hate the Government. . . . He may be of use."

The watchman went away, and a few minutes later opened the door and let in a rather short, lean old man with thick hair, a thin, grizzly goat's beard, and kindly weary blue eyes.

" What do you want ?" asked Mezhenétsky.

The old man glanced at him, and quickly dropping his eyes again, held out his small, thin but energetic hand.

" What do you want ?"

" I want a word with thee."

" What word ?"

" About faith."

" What faith ?"

" They say thou art of the same faith as that youth that Antichrist's servants strangled with a rope in Odessa."

" What youth ?"

" Him as they strangled in Odessa in the autumn."

" Svetlogoúb, I suppose ?"

" Yes, the same. . . . Thy friend ?" At every question the old man gave Mezhenétsky's face a searching glance with his kind eyes, and at once dropped them again.

" Yes, we were closely bound to each other."

" And of the same faith ? . . ."

" The same, I expect . . ." Mezhenétsky answered, with a smile.

" It's about that I want a word with thee."

" And what is it you want exactly ?"

" To know your faith."

" Our faith. Well, sit down," said Mezhenétsky, shrugging his shoulders. " This is our faith : We believe that there are men who, having seized all the power, torment and deceive the people, and that we must not spare ourselves, but must struggle against them in order to save the people they exploit." From habit Mezhenétsky used the word " exploit," but correcting himself, he substituted the word " torment " ; " and so they must be destroyed. They kill, and so they must be killed, until they come to their senses."

The old sectarian sighed, without raising his eyes.

" Our faith lies in not sparing ourselves, and in abolishing despotic Government, and establishing a free, elected, popular Government."

The old man heaved a deep sigh ; rose, smoothed the skirts of his gown, sank down on his knees, and knocking his forehead on the dirty floor, lay at Mezhenétsky's feet.

" Why are you bowing ?"

" Do not deceive me !   Reveal to me wherein your faith lies," said the old man, without rising or lifting his head.

" I have told you wherein our faith lies.   But get up, or else I won't talk."

The old man rose.

" And did that youth hold the same faith ?" he said, standing before Mezhenétsky and glancing at him now and then with his kind eyes, and immediately dropping them again.

" Yes, it was . . . just that.   That is why they hanged him.   And me, you see, they are taking to the Petropávlof Fortress for the same faith."

The old man made a deep bow and went out of the cell.   " Not therein lay that youth's faith," he thought.   " That youth knew the true faith, but this one either just boasts that he holds the same faith, or he won't reveal it. . . . Well, what of that ?   I will go on striving. . . . Here or in Siberia, and everywhere, there is God, and everywhere there are men.   If you've lost your way, ask it ;" and the old man took the New Testament, which opened of itself at the pages of Revelation; and, having put on his spectacles, he sat down by the window and began to read.

IX

Another seven years passed. Mezhenétsky had served his sentence of solitary confinement in the Petropávlof Fortress, and was being transported to penal servitude in Siberia.

During those seven years he had lived through a great deal, but the trend of his thoughts had not changed, nor had his energy weakened. When cross-examined before his imprisonment in the Fortress, he had astonished the magistrates and judges by his firmness and his scornful attitude with regard to the people in whose power he found himself. In the depths of his soul he suffered because he had been caught and was unable to finish the work he had begun ; but he did not show it. As soon as he was face to face with people, the energy of anger awoke in him. He remained silent when questioned, except when an opportunity presented itself to say something that would wound one of the examiners : a gendarme officer, or the Public Prosecutor.

When the usual phrase, " You can materially better your position by a frank confession," was repeated to him, he smiled contemptuously and said, after a short pause :

" If you expect to make me betray my com-

rades, through fear or for profit, you are judging
me by yourselves. Can you possibly imagine
that when doing what you are now trying me for,
I was not prepared for the worst ? So you cannot surprise or frighten me by anything you do ;
you can do to me what you like, but I shall not
speak."

He was pleased to see how, quite abashed, they
glanced at one another.

In the Petropávlof Fortress he was put into
a small damp cell with a window high up in the
wall, and he knew that it was not for months, but
for years, and was seized with terror at the well-
ordered, dead silence and by the consciousness
that he was not alone, but that behind these
impenetrable walls were other prisoners, sentenced to ten or twenty years' confinement,
committing suicide, being hanged, going out of
their minds, or slowly dying of consumption.
Here were men and women and friends, perhaps. . . . "Years will pass, and I too shall lose
my reason, hang myself, or die. And no one will
ever hear of it," he thought.

Anger rose in his soul, against everybody, but
especially against those who were the cause of his
imprisonment. This anger demanded objects to
wreck itself on, demanded action and noise—but

here was dead silence, or the soft footsteps of silent men who answered no questions, and the sound of doors being locked or unlocked, food brought at appointed hours, visits from the silent men, the light of the rising sun shining through the dim panes, then darkness; and the same silence, and the same footsteps, and the same sounds, to-day and to-morrow. . . . And his anger, unable to vent itself, ate into his heart.

He tried to tap, but was not answered, and his tapping was followed only by the same soft footsteps, and the calm voice of a man threatening him with the punishment cell.

Only sleep brought rest and relief; but the awakening was all the more dreadful. In his dreams he always saw himself free, and generally absorbed in actions he considered incompatible with Revolutionary activity. Sometimes he was playing some strange kind of violin, sometimes courting girls, or rowing in a boat, or hunting, or having a doctor's degree conferred on him by some foreign University for a strange scientific discovery, and returning thanks in a speech at a dinner-party. These dreams were so distinct, and the reality so dull and monotonous, that they differed little from actuality.

The only painful thing about his dreams was

that he always woke up at the very moment that what he was striving for and longing for was on the point of being realized. With a sudden heart-pang all the pleasant circumstances would vanish, and only the torment of unfulfilled desires remained. And again there was the grey wall with the damp marks, lit up by a small lamp, and under his body the hard plank bed, with the hay all pushed to one side in the sack which served for a mattress. The pleasantest time was when he was asleep ; but the longer he was in prison, the less he slept. He waited for sleep as for the greatest happiness : he longed for it, and the more he longed, the wider awake he became. He needed only to ask himself, " Am I falling asleep ?" for his drowsiness to vanish.

Running about and jumping in his cage did not help. Active exercise only brought on weakness and excited his nerves ; the crown of his head began to ache, and he had but to shut his eyes to see faces appearing on a dark, spangled background — shaggy, bald, large-mouthed, crooked-mouthed—each more horrible than the rest. These faces made most terrifying grimaces. Later on they began to appear when his eyes were open, and not only the faces, but whole figures chattering and dancing. He grew terrified, jumped up, knocked his head against the wall, and screamed. Then the slot in the door would open :

" Screaming is forbidden !" a calm, monotonous voice would remark.

" Call the inspector !" shouted Mezhenétsky. He received no answer, and the slot was again closed. And such despair would seize him that he longed for one thing only—death. Once, when in such a state, he decided to take his life. There was a ventilator in the cell, to which a rope with a noose could be fastened, and by getting on to the bedstead it would be possible to hang oneself. But he had no rope. He began to tear his sheet into strips, but there were not enough of them.

Then he decided to starve himself, and did not eat for two days ; but on the third he became quite weak, and had a worse fit of hallucinations. When food was brought him he lay with open eyes, but unconscious, on the floor. The doctor came, laid him on the bed, and gave him rum and morphia, and he fell asleep.

When he awoke next morning, the doctor was standing by him, shaking his head. And suddenly Mezhenétsky was seized by the stimulating sensation of anger, which he had long not felt.

" How is it you are not ashamed to serve here ?"
he said, as the doctor, with bowed head, counted
his pulse. " Why are you doctoring me, only to
torment me again ? Why, it is just the same as
standing at a flogging and giving permission to
repeat the operation !"

" Be so good as to turn round on your back,"
the doctor said, quite unruffled, and, without
looking at him, took out of his side-pocket the
instruments for sounding him.

" They used to heal the wounds, in order that
the remaining five thousand strokes could be
given ! . . . Go to the devil ! Go to hell !" he
suddenly exclaimed, taking his legs off the bed.
" Be off ! . . . I'll die without you !"

" That's not right, young man. . . . We know
an answer for rudeness. . . ."

" To the devil, to the devil !" and Mezhenétsky
was so terrible that the doctor hurried away.

X

Whether it was a result of the medicine he took,
or that he had passed a crisis, or that his anger
against the doctor cured him, at any rate from
then onwards Mezhenétsky took himself in hand
and started quite a new life.

" They can't and won't keep me here for ever,"
he thought. " After all, they will liberate me some
time. Perhaps—and very likely—there will be a
change of Administration (our people are working),
and therefore I must take care of my life, to go out
strong, healthy, and able to continue the work."

He took a long time to consider the best way
of living to attain his object ; and this was how
he arranged matters. He went to bed at nine,
and whether he slept or not, remained in bed
till 5 a.m. Then he got up, made himself tidy,
washed, did gymnastics, and then, as he said to
himself, went to business. In imagination he
walked through the streets of Petersburg, from
the Névsky to the Nadézhdinsky, trying to picture
to himself all he was likely to see on his way :
signboards, houses, policemen, carriages, and the
people he might meet. In the Nadézhdinsky
Street he entered the house of an acquaintance
and fellow-worker, and there, with him and
other comrades who dropped in, discussed pros-
pects for the future. They argued, disputed :
Mezhenétsky speaking for himself and the others.
Sometimes he spoke aloud, and then the sentinel
made remarks to him through the window in the
door ; but Mezhenétsky paid no heed to him,
and continued his imaginary day in Petersburg.

After spending a couple of hours with his comrade, he returned home to dinner, dined—first in imagination and then in reality, on the food that was brought him—and always ate moderately. Then, again in imagination, he sat at home, sometimes studying history and sometimes mathematics, and sometimes on Sundays literature. Studying history meant choosing a certain period and nation, and recalling all the facts and the chronology belonging to them. The study of mathematics meant working out and mentally solving problems. (He was particularly fond of this occupation.) On Sundays he recalled Poúshkin, Gógol, Shakespeare, or himself composed something.

Before going to bed, he again went for a short imaginary walk; carried on amusing, merry and sometimes serious conversations with comrades, both men and women—some that had really taken place and some that were newly invented. And so it went on till bedtime ; and just before lying down he really walked two thousand steps backwards and forwards in his cage for exercise, and when in bed he generally slept.

It was the same the next day. Sometimes he travelled south, and went about inciting the people and arranging riots, and with the people, expelled the landlords and divided the land among the peasants. All this, however, he did not imagine all at once, but gradually, going into every detail. In his fancy the Revolutionary parties always triumphed ; the power of the Government grew weaker, and it was obliged to call together a Council. The Imperial family and all the oppressors of the people disappeared, and a Republic was established, and he, Mezhenétsky, was chosen President. Sometimes he reached this climax too quickly, and then he began again from the beginning, and attained his end by other means.

So he lived one, two, three years : occasionally discontinuing this rigorous order of life for a time, but always returning to it again. Fits of insomnia and visions of horrible faces rarely troubled him now, and when they did, he looked at the ventilator and pictured to himself how he would fasten a rope to it, make a noose, and hang himself. He managed to master these fits, and they never lasted long.

Thus he spent nearly seven years. When his term of imprisonment came to an end, and he started on his way to penal servitude in Siberia, he was quite healthy, fresh, and in perfect possession of his mental faculties.

XI

As he was a criminal of special importance, he was conveyed separately, and not allowed to communicate with others ; and it was only in the prison at Krasnoyársk that he first succeeded in having some intercourse with other political prisoners who were also being sent to penal servitude. There were six of them : two women and four men. They were all young people of a new type unfamiliar to Mezhenétsky. They were Revolutionists of a newer generation— his successors—and therefore of special interest to him. Mezhenétsky expected to find them following in his footsteps, and therefore valuing very highly what had been done by their fore-runners, and especially by himself, Mezhenétsky. He was prepared to treat them with kindness and condescension, but he had the unpleasant sur-prise of discovering that these young people not only did not regard him as a pioneer and teacher, but treated him with something like condescen-sion, evading and excusing his superannuated opinions. According to the views of these new Revolutionists, all that Mezhenétsky and his friends had done—all their attempts to rouse the peasants, and especially their terroristic methods

and their assassinations of the Governor Krop-
ótkin, Mezentsóf, and even of Alexander II, had
been a series of mistakes. They had all merely
contributed to the triumph of the reaction under
Alexander III, which put society back almost
to the days of serfdom. According to them, the
true path was a quite different one.

For two days and the greater part of two nights
the disputes between Mezhenétsky and his new
acquaintances hardly ceased. Especially one of
them, their leader, Román (everybody called him
by his Christian name), pained and grieved
Mezhenétsky by his unwavering assurance of
being right, and by a contemptuous and even
sarcastic rejection of all the old methods of
Mezhenétsky and his comrades.

According to Román, the peasants were a
rough mob, a rabble. And with the peasants
in their present stage of development, nothing
could be done. All efforts to raise the Russian
people were like attempts to set a stone or a piece
of ice alight. The people had to be educated and
trained for solidarity, and only large industries,
and the growth of a Socialistic organization based
thereon, could accomplish this.

The land was not only unnecessary to the people,
but it was just the land that, both in Russia and

in the rest of Europe, made them Conservatives
and slaves. And he quoted the opinion of various
authorities and gave statistics, which he knew by
heart. The people must be liberated from the
land, and the sooner this is done the better. The
more of them go into factories, and the more land
the capitalists get into their hands, and the more
they oppress the people, the better. Despotism
—and especially capitalism—can only be brought
to an end by the solidarity of the workers, and
this can be attained only by trade-unions and
corporations of working men—*i.e.*, only when the
masses cease to own land, and become proletarians.

Mezhenétsky argued, and grew excited. A
dark, rather good-looking brunette, with much
hair and very brilliant eyes, irritated him particularly, as, sitting on the window-sill and hardly
taking any direct part in the conversation, she
occasionally put in a few words confirming
Román's arguments, or merely smiled contemptuously at Mezhenétsky's remarks.

" Is it possible to change all the country
labourers into factory hands ?" said Mezhenétsky.

" Why not ?" retorted Román. " It is a
general economic law."

" How do we know it to be general ?" said
Mezhenétsky.

"Read Kautsky!" remarked the dark woman, with a contemptuous smile.

"Even granting (though I don't grant it) that the people will be changed into proletarians," said Mezhenétsky, "what makes you suppose that they will take the form you have foreordained?"

"Because it is a scientific deduction," put in the dark woman, turning away from the window.

When the kind of activity necessary to attain their aim came under discussion, their differences became even more accentuated. Román and his friends insisted on the necessity of educating an army of workmen to help in the transformation of the peasants into factory workers, and to preach Socialism among them, and not only to refrain from openly fighting the Government, but to use it for the attainment of their aims. Mezhenétsky, on the contrary, declared that one must fight the Government openly and terrorize it; since the Government was both stronger and more cunning than they. "It is not you that will deceive the Government—but you that will be deceived by it. We carried on propaganda work among the people and resisted the Government as well."

"And much good you did!" said the dark woman.

" Yes, I do think that open warfare with the Government is a waste of energy," remarked Román.

" March the First* a waste of energy !" shouted Mezhenétsky. " We sacrificed ourselves, our lives—and you sit quietly at home, enjoying yourselves, and only preach !"

" We don't enjoy ourselves very much," said Román, glancing round at his comrades, and burst into a fit of not infectious but loud, clear and self-assured laughter.

The brunette shook her head, smiling ironically.

" We don't enjoy ourselves much," repeated Román ; " and if we sit here we owe it to the reaction, and the reaction is the outcome of that very First of March !"

Mezhenétsky was silent.   He felt himself choking with anger, and went out into the corridor.

XII

Trying to master his excitement, Mezhenétsky began pacing up and down the corridor. The doors of the cells were left open till the evening roll-call. A tall, fair-haired convict, with a face

* Alexander II was assassinated on March the First (O.S.), 1881.

the kindly expression of which was not destroyed by the shaving of half his head, approached Mezhenétsky.

"There's a convict here in our cell—he has seen your Honour, and he says to me : ' Call him here ' !"

"What convict ?"

" ' Snuff-rule ' is what we call him—an old man, a sectarian. He says : ' Tell that man to come to me.' He means your Honour."

"Where is he ?"

"Why, here, in our cell. ' Call that gentleman !' he says."

Mezhenétsky followed the convict into a rather small cell, where several prisoners were sitting and lying on the bunks.

There at the edge of the bunk on the bare boards, under his grey prison cloak, lay the same old sectarian who, seven years before, had come to ask Mezhenétsky about Svetlogoúb. The old man's face was pale, emaciated and quite shrivelled up ; his hair was still just as thick ; his upturned, thin, short beard quite white ; and his blue eyes kindly and attentive. He lay on his back, evidently feverish, and his cheek-bones were an unhealthy red.

Mezhenétsky came up to him.

" What do you want ?" he asked.

The old man painfully raised himself on his elbow and held out his small, thin, trembling hand. Preparing to speak, he first breathed heavily, and drawing breath with difficulty, began in a low voice :

" Thou wouldst not reveal it to me that time . . . may God be with thee, but I reveal it to everybody !"

" Reveal what ?"

" About the Lamb. . . . I reveal about the Lamb . . . that youth had the Lamb. And it is written that the Lamb will overcome—overcome all. And those that are with him, they are the chosen, and the faithful. . . ."

" I do not understand," said Mezhenétsky.

" Thou must understand in the spirit. The kings and the beast . . . the Lamb shall overcome them."

" What kings ?" Mezhenétsky asked.

" There are seven kings : five are fallen, and one is, and the other one is not yet come ; and when he cometh he must continue a short space. . . . That means, his end will come soon. Have you understood ?"

Mezhenétsky shook his head, thinking the old man was delirious and his words meaningless.

His fellow-convicts thought so too. The shaven convict, who had called Mezhenétsky, came up, and nudging his elbow to draw his attention, looked at the old man with a wink.

" Always chattering, always chattering, our ' Snuff-rule '! What about, he don't know himself !"

So thought Mezhenétsky and the old man's fellow-convicts, as they looked at him ; yet the old man knew very well what he was saying, and for him it had a clear, deep meaning. He meant that evil was not to reign much longer, but that the Lamb was overcoming all by righteousness and meekness, and that the Lamb would dry every tear, and there would be no more hangmen, nor sickness, nor death. And he felt that this was already happening—happening all over the world, that it was happening in his soul, enlightened by the nearness of death.

" Ay, come quickly. . . . Amen ! Even so, come, Lord Jesus !" said he, with a faint, significant, and as Mezhenétsky thought, insane smile.

XIII

" And that's a representative of the people !" thought Mezhenétsky, as he left the old man.

" And he is one of the best of them—and such ignorance ! . . . They say " (he was thinking of Román and his friends) " that with the people as they are now, nothing can be done."

At one time Mezhenétsky had carried on his Revolutionary activity among the peasants, and was therefore aware of the " inertia," as he called it, of the Russian folk. He had met soldiers, some in service and some discharged, and knew their tenacious, obtuse belief in the validity of oaths and the necessity of submission ; as well as the impossibility of influencing them by arguments. He knew all this, but had never arrived at the conclusion which should have been the evident outcome of that knowledge.

His talk with the Revolutionists had troubled and irritated him. " They say that all we have done — what Haltoúrin, Kibáltchitch, Sophie Peróvsky did—was unnecessary, and even harmful ; and that we caused the reaction of Alexander III's time . . . that, thanks to us, the people are convinced that the whole Revolutionary movement comes from landlords, who killed the Tsar because he took the serfs from them ! What rubbish ! What a want of understanding, and what insolence to imagine it !" he thought, continuing to pace the corridor. All

the cells had now been closed, except the one
where the new Revolutionists were. As he
drew near he heard the laughter of the dark
woman who was so antipathetic to him, and the
rasping, determined sound of Román's voice.
Román was saying :

"... unable to understand the laws of economy,
they took no account of what they were doing.
And in a great measure it was . . ."

Mezhenétsky could not, and did not wish to,
hear what was "in a great measure," nor did he
need to know it. The tone of voice of the man
was sufficient to show in what utter contempt
they held him, Mezhenétsky, the hero of the
Revolution, who had sacrificed twelve years of
his life to the cause.

And in Mezhenétsky's heart there arose such
dreadful hatred as he had never experienced
before—hatred of everybody and everything—of
all this senseless world in which only people who
are like animals can live—people such as the old
man with his "Lamb," and semi-animal hangmen and gaolers, and insolent, self-assured, still-
born dogmatists.

The warder on duty came in and led the
women away to the women's quarters. Mezhenétsky went to the other end of the corridor

so as not to meet him. The warder came back and locked the cell of the new political prisoners, and suggested to Mezhenétsky that he should go back to his own. Mezhenétsky obeyed mechanically, but asked that his door should not be locked.

In his cell, Mezhenétsky lay down on the bunk with his face to the wall.

Was it possible that all his powers had been wasted : his energy, his strength of will, his genius (he did not consider anyone above him in mental qualities) wasted for nothing ? He remembered the letter he had received quite lately, when already on his way to Siberia, from Svetlogoúb's mother, reproaching him ("like a woman," stupidly, as he thought) for having led her son to perdition by drawing him into the terrorist activity. When he received that letter he had only smiled contemptuously ; what could that stupid woman understand of the aims that stood before him and Svetlogoúb ? But now, when he recalled the letter and Svetlogoúb's sweet, trusting, affectionate nature, he began to muse : first about Svetlogoúb, and then about himself. Could his whole life have been a mistake ? He closed his eyes and tried to fall asleep, but was horrified to find that the state he had

been in during his first month in the Petropávlof Fortress had again returned. Again he
felt the pain in the crown of his head, again he
saw faces with enormous mouths, shaggy and
terrible, on a dark background, speckled with
little stars; and again forms appeared before
his open eyes. There was only this new about
it : he saw a criminal with shaved head and grey
trousers swinging before him, and by a sequence
of ideas he began to look for a ventilator to which
he could attach a rope. Intolerable hatred that
demanded expression, burned in Mezhenétsky's
heart. He could not lie still, could not grow
calm, and could not get rid of his thoughts.

"How ?" he began to ask himself. "By
cutting an artery ? I might not succeed. . . .
Hanging ? . . . Of course ! That's the sim-
plest !" He remembered that he had seen a
bundle of logs tied together by a cord in the
corridor. "Get up on the logs, or on a stool ?
. . . The watchman is pacing up and down the
corridor, but he will fall asleep or go away. . . .
I shall have to wait, and then take the rope and
fasten it to the ventilator."

Standing at his door, Mezhenétsky listened to
the watchman's steps, and now and then, when
the latter was at the far end of the corridor, he

looked out through the chink. But the watchman did not go away nor fall asleep, and still Mezhenétsky listened eagerly to the sound of his footsteps, and waited.

At the same time, in the cell where the sick old man lay in complete darkness but for a smoky lamp, amid the sleepy sounds of night—breathing, groaning, snoring, coughing—the greatest of life's events was taking place. The old sectarian was dying; and to his spiritual vision was revealed all that he had so desired during his whole life. In the midst of dazzling light he saw the Lamb in the shape of a radiant youth, and a great multitude of people of all nations standing before him clothed in white; and they all rejoiced that there was no more evil on earth. All this was happening in his own soul and in the whole world, as the old man knew, and he was filled with a great joy and peace.

But the others in the cell knew nothing of it, and heard only the death-rattle in the old man's throat; and his neighbour awoke and roused the others, and when the rattle ceased and the old man's body grew cold, his fellow-inmates knocked at the door.

The watchman came in, and ten minutes later two convicts carried the lifeless body out of the

cell and down to the mortuary. The watchman followed them out and locked the outside door after him. The corridor was left
empty.

"Lock up, lock up!" thought Mezhenétsky,
who from his door had followed all that went on.
"You will not prevent me from escaping from
all these horrors!"

Mezhenétsky no longer felt the inward terror
that had hitherto oppressed him; he was absorbed
by only one thought : the fear of being prevented
from carrying out his intention.

With beating heart he went out, and reaching
the logs, undid the cord that bound them together, and drew it from under the bundle ;
then, looking round at the outer door, he took
the cord into his cell. There he got on to the
stool, threw the cord over the ventilator, and,
having tied the ends together, made a noose out
of the double cord. It hung too low. He altered
this and again made a noose, measured it round
his neck, and anxiously listening and looking
towards the door, again got onto the stool, put
his head into the noose, adjusted it, kicked away
the stool, and remained hanging.

It was only when making his morning round
that the warder noticed Mezhenétsky standing,

with his legs bent at the knees, beside the stool, which lay on its side.

He was taken down, and the prison inspector came running, and, hearing that Román was a physician, called him to give his aid to the strangled man.

All the usual remedies were administered to bring him back to life, but Mezhenétsky did not come to.

His body was carried down to the mortuary, and laid beside the body of the old sectarian.

1906.

THE END